THE

C O R S A I R ;

OR,

T HE FOUNDLING OF THE SEA.

𝔄 𝔯𝔬𝔪𝔞𝔫𝔠𝔢.

BY HARRY HAZEL.

LONDON:

PUBLISHED BY G. PURKESS, COMPTON-
STREET, SOHO; STRANGE, PATERNOSTER-ROW;

THE CORSAIR;

OR,

THE FOUNDLING OF THE SEA.
A Romance.

BY HARRY HAZEL.

CHAPTER I.

A CALM ON THE ATLANTIC.—THE "SPARTA" AND HER CREW.—THE STRANGE PASSENGER.—HIS INTERVIEW WITH FANNY FLOYD.—DARING FEAT OF EDWARD DUVALLE.—HIS MYSTERIOUS CONDUCT.

IT was a calm and beautiful night in the year 182—, there was no moon, but the stars shone out from the blue vault above with that brightness which can only be

No. 1.

seen in the trophies, almost supplying the deficiency of light caused by the absence of the queen of night. Not a breath of air rippled the mighty waters of the Atlantic, which seemed like a vast mirror of burnished steel, reflecting with peculiar clearness the diamond-studded canopy above.

Upon the glassy sea a noble ship was becalmed, and as she lay as motionless and majestic as a palace founded upon a rock. Her canvass was all set, but it hung loosely to her yards, and the helmsman paced to and fro the quarter-deck, deeming that under such a pacific state of things, a constant attention at the wheel was quite unnecessary. Still he did not entirely desert his post, but remained near it, and occasionally looked over the taffrail, and watched the sportiveness of the dolphins as they flitted to and fro about the stern of the vessel.

The ship was the "Sparta," of and from Baltimore, and bound to the Rio de Plata; and although she had been twenty-five days at sea, her passage was not yet half completed, owing to a protracted calm; it having already lasted ten days, and during the whole time the ship had not made three degrees of latitude; and she would have made less, had not the boats been out towing the ship slowly along for three or four of the last days of the calm.

A group of merry-hearted seamen were idling away the evening watch, upon the forward deck, spinning yarns, singing songs, and indulging in other diversions peculiar alone to those who follow the trackless ocean.

"Come, my hearties, can't you whistle us up a breeze?" said Bill Rattlin, an active looking tar, to the group of sailors, as he came forth from the forecastle.

"For my part," replied one of the number, "I'm blowed if I've got breath enough in my body to blow out the binnacle light."

"Captain Wingate 'll have the boats out again to-morrow, sure," resumed the first speaker; "if we don't prevail on Boreas to stir up old Neptune, and get the Sparta out o' this dead calm."

"Captain Windgate be d——d!" replied an athletic seaman, in a gruff voice, as he ejected a huge quid of tobacco from his mouth with sufficient force to lodge it between the bright twinklers of the black cook, who was seated upon a coil of rigging, quietly listening to the conversation.

"What's dat? Who frow'd dat ar?" demanded black Pete, with frowning indignation, as the nauseous masticated weed came in contact with his flat organ of smelling.

Pete's inquiry was not taken the slightest notice of, and the sailors continued conversation, supposing that from his apparently mild and forgiving disposition he would not resent it, as he had often been made subject of indignities of a like nature, which he could not or dared not avenge. But Pete's character was not so well understood by his shipmates as it was by himself; and he was well assured who it was that committed the ungentlemanly outrage upon his person, but he assumed ignorance, as he did not deem that that was an opportune time to repay the insult. A time would come, he inwardly resolved, when he should return it four-fold, particularly upon "Big Tom," as the burly sailor was denominated by the ship's crew. With a sullen and dogged air, the negro left his unpleasant associates and entered his caboose, where we shall leave him brooding over his afflictions.

It was not yet ten o' clock, and while a portion of the ship's crew still remained in the vicinity of the windlass, two persons came forth from the cabin to enjoy the beauties of the night who require from us more than a passing notice, as they are destined to act something more prominent than supernumerary characters in our romantic narrative, and perhaps deserve the appellations of hero and heroine. The latter was leaning somewhat timidly upon the arm of the former as they came upon the deck, and seemed to be well satisfied with each other's society, as may be supposed from the fact that one was a gentleman of about twenty-two years of age, of prepossessing appearance, with an expressive and intelligently-marked countenance, while the other was a charming young lady just verging into womanhood, graceful as a sylph, and lovely as the goddess of beauty. Fanny Floyd—for oy this name our heroine is to be known—was the daughter of a rich planter residing near St. Inigoes, in the state of Maryland, who, with her father, had embarked on board the good Sparta, as passengers for Rio Janeiro, where they intended to spend some months with connections of Mr. Floyd, he having married a Spanish lady in that city, some twenty years previous, and the only fruit of their union was the fair Fanny—her mother having died while she was yet in her infancy.

Mr. Floyd, at the time we are writing, was an invalid, and this was his great inducement in visiting a more salubrious climate, that he might escape the unhealthful effects which another northern winter might have upon his constitution. It was at the suggestion and the solicitations of Miss Fanny that she was permitted to accompany him, and the invalid father had already felt the comforts of her ministering hand, during the time they had been at sea. They had brought with them two faithful slaves, one a female and the other a male, which had been reared upon Mr. Floyd's plantation, in Maryland, and who devoted themselves assiduously to the wants of their master and young mistress.

The young man whom we find on terms of intimacy with Miss Floyd, was an agreeable and intelligent gentleman, and had booked his name among the list of passengers of the Sparta, as Edward Duvalle. Farther than this concerning him, was unknown to any of the ship's company, except that his pleasing and winning, manners had gained him the esteem of all on board; and farther than this will not be divulged to our readers at this time, trusting that they will have sufficient patience to follow us through the incidents of our tale, in the course of which his character will be clearly developed. It may appear singular to some, under these circumstances, that he should be found so intimate with Miss Floyd, all of which too, was well known to her father. The cause of this may be explained in a short narrative of events which had but recently occurred.

At the time of the Sparta's departure from the wharf, Mr. Floyd's family, unfortunately, was not on board, but before the ship had got beyond hailing distance, a carriage drove down to the wharf, a signal was raised, and the vessel backed her topsails, and hove to, for the purpose of taking on board her tardy passengers. The wind at the time was blowing almost a gale from the north-west, and some difficulty occurred in procuring a suitable boat to put off with the newly arrived passengers, and a large quautity of baggage. One of inferior size was at length obtained, and so great was the turbulence of the waters when the boat reached the ship's side, that it was with the greatest difficulty that they were enabled to assist Mr. Floyd (being, as we before stated an invalid) on board the ship. Fanny, in attempting too hastily to follow her father, lost her footing, and was precipitated into the waves. A piercing shriek was heard above the raging elements, and the word was quickly passed along the deck of the ship that a female was overboard, and amid the confusion the weak voice of Mr. Floyd was heard in lamentable and heart-rending tones, saying,

"Save, oh save my beloved daughter!"

The old man, in spite of the resistance of several of those standing by to prevent his rushing to certain destruction, would have thrown himself over the ship's side in the vain attempt to save her, had not a young man who was standing near, anticipated his intentions by rushing past him and leaping into the water to rescue the drowning girl. In one short moment he would have been too late—he seized her by her long flowing hair and held her above the surface with one hand, while with the other he was enabled to keep himself up until a rope was thrown him, which he contrived to fasteu round his body, and was thus drawn towards the ship, and finally to the gang-way, which he ascended with the exhausted Miss Floyd in his arms.

This remarkable and daring feat of humanity was the chief topic of conversation on board of the ship, and when Miss Floyd had entirely recovered, she begged to see her noble preserver, and to acknowledge to him in person, her grateful thanks. Edward Duvalle was accordingly conducted to the cabin, where the lady and her father improved the opportunity of making their acknowledgments. As he was about to retire, Mr. Floyd begged him to tarry for one moment, and to excuse him or a temporary absence. He presently returned and offered him as a token of his regard a magnificently jewelled watch, which Duvalle posively refused, averring that he had been amply repaid by the attention which the had shown to one who was and must continue a stranger to them.

"At least," said Fanny, taking from her finger a ring with a large vignette attached to it, "you will accept of this little token for my sake."

The manner in which this was said and done was irresistible to the susceptible feelings of Duvalle. He graciously took the ring, placed it upon his finger, and said,

"Yes, for your sake I cannot refuse."

After this incident, Edward and Fanny first met occasionally upon the deck of the noble ship. As each day passed away they seemed more in each other's company, until at length, it was rare that one could be seen minus the company of the other.

In this relation matters stood upon the evening mentioned at the beginning of this chapter, and it is therefore not strange at all, that they should cherish towards each other, sentiments of the highest esteem, if not of affection. Some insight in regard to the opinions held by each may be gathered from the annexed singular conversation, which took place as soon as they had had seated themselves in a somewhat retired position upon the quarter deck of the vessel.

"Tell me, Edward," said she, "why it is that you seem so melancholy since we have become acquainted? During our first interview you were happy as I could hope ever to see you."

"Do I seem unhappy now, Fanny?" asked he in tones of sober earnestness, and while there was no animation or joy visible in his countenance.

"Indeed you do; and the serious tones of your voice, so pleasant but a few day ago, now almost chill me."

"I confess, Fanny, as it is useless for me to dissemble, that there is good and abundant cause for my grief."

"You surprise me," said Miss Floyd, as she looked up into his face with a startled but timid expression. "What possible event could have occurred within the narrow limits of this ship that should give you one moment's pain?"

"Nothing—yes—much!" he stammered in reply.

There was a pause for several moments, and the young man seemed deeply affected when he saw that Fanny's eyes were wet with tears.

"Let me be plain but brief, Miss Floyd."

"Nay, nay, not brief. Let me know all; but pardon my inquisitiveness," said she. "And do not, I beseech you, Edward, address me on terms of coldness."

"God forbid that I should ever have cause so to do; but in reality I do you a serious wrong when I address you with language better befitting a lover than a stranger."

"Why will you persist in calling yourself a stranger. Have not the many hours which we have been permitted to be together, been sufficient at least to rank me as one of your acquaintances? And did you not save my life at the imminent risk of your own?"

"Say no more of that, Fanny;" replied Duvalle. "I grant, dear girl, that in the common acceptation of the term, we are intimate acquaintances and friends; but that implies not that you know him you appears before you as Edward Duvalle."

"Not know you? How, Edward, what can you mean?" questioned Fanny with mysterious apprehension.

"I mean that he whom you know as Edward Duvalle—who has passed many happy hours in your sweet society—who will confess boldly and freely that he loves Fanny Floyd with all the warmth of his affections—is yet and must ever be a stranger to you."

"Oh, Heavens!" exclaimed Fanny, "I cannot understand; and yet I fear—"

"Yes; and you have good grounds for fearing that Edward Duvalle is not the character that has been assigned him by this ship's company. Lady, would to

God I could unfold to you my true standing in the world, but that at the present time is impossible. Should I ever be so fortunate as to make good one resolution I have formed, then, and not till then, will I appear before you and the world in my true person."

Fanny burst into tears. "I can trust you. I can have nothing to fear from one like you," said she sobbingly.

"I would not, my sweet girl, give you one moment's pain; nor would I be guilty of using the slightest deception in gaining your esteem. I can only regret that I did not sooner put you upon your guard, but since I first saw you I have been indulging in your sweet smiles until I have become intoxicated with an ardent passion. Indeed, I am bound by a spell of fascination. But I have yet power to break it, though my heart be sundered in the effort. Ere many days we shall part—in all probability never to meet again, but I shall never forget the happy moments I have passed in this ship—and I shall likewise cherish in my memory the bright being who has caused me so much felicity."

"Nay, nay, Edward, talk not thus. Surely in you there can be no guile."

"I know, sweet Fanny, your confiding and generous disposition. I know your purity and inestimable worth; and would to God that I was worthy of the sentiments you have revealed to me; that I might here bend the knee and offer you my heart and hand, and feel that I was not imposing upon the good and virtuous. But this precious boon is denied me; and were the mysterious veil, by which my true character is concealed, raised, you would regard me with indignation if not with horror; therefore, gentle creature, this had better be our last interview, and although there is a possibility of my remaining on board of this ship some days longer, our pleasant intimacy had better be discontinued. If I am right in my information and conjectures, an event will ere long take place which will not only separate us for ever, but reveal to you facts, startling indeed, and which may serve to unfold to you the reason why I cannot, with any degree of propriety, seek to cultivate an intimacy happily begun, but which, alas, if persevered in, must lead to unpleasant if not disastrous results."

Duvalle uttered these words with all the complacency that he could command, but it was evident from his quivering lip, his forced utterance and energetic manner, that he was deeply moved. Fanny trembled like an aspen leaf, and tears gushed copiously from her eyes. She looked up in his face but her heart was too full to speak.

"Go, Fanny to your father," resumed Duvalle. "Tell him that I am unworthy of your regard."

"No—no—Edward, this must not be," replied she sobbingly. "One so noble and frank and generous as yourself, cannot be other than he seems."

"And yet to be more plain, I am allied to that which is ignoble, base, and criminal; and oh, that the time might come when I should be for ever disenthralled from a dreadful alliance which weighs my very soul to the earth. Perhaps that time may come, but the path before me looks gloomy and dark, and in that path lurks danger, terrific and bloody."

Duvalle could say no more; but taking the hand of the beautiful Fanny, he led her to the entrance of the ladies' cabin, and bidding her 'good night,' retired to his own state-room.

At this time the group of sailors forward had mostly dispersed, and none were left upon the Sparta's deck except those who kept the night-watch.

Duvalle again for a few moments appeared on the quarter-deck of the ship, bearing a night-glass in his hand, and after surveying the sleeping sea in every direction, and discovering nothing, he returned to his quarters, where we shall leave him for a few hours, not in a state of repose, but brooding over a dreadful event, which he believed was near at hand.

CHAPTER II.

A SAIL DESCRIBED.—HER SUSPICIOUS APPEARANCE.—CAPTAIN WINGATE AND THE MATE OF THE "SPARTA."—ALARM OF THE LATTER.—INTERVIEW WITH EDWARD DUVALLE.—HIS CORROBORATION OF THE CAPTAIN'S OPINION IN REGARD TO THE CHASE.—THE BOXES OF MUSKETS.—THE STRANGE SAIL A PIRATE.

THE night wore away and the calm continued, and there was as little prospect of a breeze as there had been on the preceding morning. The mate came upon deck and issued orders to man the boats as soon as the crew had partaken of their morning meal. This caused, as might be presumed, from the remark of Big Tom on the night previous, no little dissatisfaction among the sailors; and, it is certain that almost a mutiny would have been raised had not the cry of—

"Sail ho;" from the look-out on the foretopsail yard, at that moment interrupted the progress of dissension and disobedience which was evidently increasing among the foremast-men.

"Where-a-away!" sung out the mate.

"On our lee-quarter, sir," answered the man from aloft.

"What do you make her out to be?"

"A large clipper-built schooner."

"What is her course?"

"She is now directly in our wake—she has two boats out fully manned."

The strange sail at the time she was descried, was about six miles astern, and in less than half an hour she had approached near enough to prove to the captain and crew of the "Sparta," that it would be good policy to avoid so suspicious a looking craft. The boats were accordingly manned, and at a snail-like pace the heavy merchantman was dragged along at the rate of one knot per hour, while it was apparent that the schooner gained upon her sufficiently fast to be broadside to her before the sun could pass the meridian.

"Mr. Cooper," said Captain Wingate, addressing the mate, apart from any of the passengers or crew; "I wish to create no unnecessary alarm, but I am fully confirmed in the belief that yon schooner making towards us is a pirate."

"It cannot be possible. A pirate has not been seen in these latitudes for many years."

"True; but I will give you the reasons for my belief," continued the captain. "I have been watching her steadily for the last hour through my glass, and if my eye does not greatly deceive me, that is the clipper-built craft which three months ago attracted so much attention in the harbour of Baltimore, and which was reported to be bound on a private expedition to Europe."

"I recollect her well," answered the mate; "but you must bear in mind that the clipper 'Vision,' was painted green with a bright scarlet streak from stem to stern, while this craft is black and has a double white streak instead of a scarlet one."

"You are correct; but it is an easy matter to alter the complexion of the hull of the vessel. Do you perceive the singular shape of her top gallant sail?" asked Mr. Wingate.

"It is peculiar, indeed."

"Well, sir, when I was having the Sparta's canvass overhauled and refitted in Baltimore, I saw that very sail upon the floor of the sailmaker's loft. I recollect distinctly making some remarks upon the singular manner in which it was cut, to the man who was at work upon it. He told me that it was intented for the clipper 'Vision,' and that it was cut in accordance with her captain's orders. Now I never saw, since I followed the sea, which is about thirty years, but one sail which corresponded with that; and if that does not prove to be the same one I will never risk my judgment upon such a matter again. This, together with the fact of her being in these latitudes, re-painted, and also from the number in the boats, and upon her deck, being four times the complement she sailed with, convinces me that she is a pirate!"

"She certainly looks suspicious," replied the mate, showing symptoms of alarm; "but what's to be done."

"Nothing, without my orders," said the captain sternly; "and on your life create no unnecessary alarm among the passengers or crew. We have two guns that can be brought to bear upon the schooner, and if our hands are not all cowards we can make at least a show of resistance. When I give the signal, clear away the guns and bring our small stock of ammunition upon deck."

"It will only exasperate the pirates if they are really such, if we make the feeble resistance that you propose," said the mate almost trembling with fear. "We shall fare the better to let them have their own way."

"Go to your duty, and remember my positive orders," said the captain, in tones of authority.

The mate left the captain, and went forward to incite the men in the boats to extra exertion.

Captain Wingate, with the aid of his glass, continued to watch the suspicious craft, as she slowly gained upon the ship.

"It is a pirate! I am positive!" exclaimed he, in tones sufficiently loud to be heard by Edward Duvalle, "who was pacing the deck near him.

"That is my opinion," said the youth, stepping up to the captain and saluting him.

"And upon what grounds do you hazard such an opinion?" inquired the captain.

"Everything indicates it, sir."

"I hope that opinion is not now prevalent on board of the ship."

"I have heard no one but yourself give utterance to that belief, sir."

"I am glad to hear it, and I would not have a single person yet entertain the belief that it is possible we may soon be attacked by pirates."

"I hope that you intend to make resistance," remarked Duvalle, with apparent concern at the captain's tardy movements.

"Yes."

"But, sir, they will be upon us before we are prepared to receive them," said the young man, impatiently.

"We have but two guns, which can be got in working order in five minutes, and if my crew and other able-bodied men on board do their duty, we can at least sell our lives dearly!"

"Excuse me, sir, for interfering at all in the affairs of your command, but a moment is approaching when more than the resources of this ship will be necessary to be brought into action to repel the fire which you will shortly have to contend with. Now, sir, you will recollect among the luggage which I sent on board of your ship there were two very heavy boxes?"

"Perfectly well."

"They contain a dozen muskets each. Another box contains several hundred rounds of cartridges with balls. They are at your service. Distribute them among the crew, and I will arm the passengers."

"You surprise me!" exclaimed Captain Wingate. "How fortunate! I will have them hoisted upon deck immediately. Hallo, there, forward! Open the main hatch and rig the tackle."

"Ay, ay, sir," was the quick response, and the forward hands went about the duty with alacrity.

The boxes of arms, fortunately, were among the last parcels of freight received, and being easily got at, were in a few moments hoisted upon the deck. As the boxes were opened and found to contain guns, the crew looked first at the weapons, then at the strange sail, and the whole truth burst suddenly upon them. In one minute every person on board of the ship knew the character of the schooner, and every preparation was made for action.

Edward Duvalle busied himself in examining each musket, and distributing them together with cartridges, alike to passengers and sailors; while at the same time the two six pounders which the ship carried on her quarter-deck were brushed up and loaded heavily with grape and canister.

At this particular juncture, as if Providence intended to favour them, a gentle breeze sprang up and the sails which had so long been useless began to fill away The boats which had been sent ahead to tow the ship, were ordered in, and the "Sparta" again under an easy press of canvass, was moving through the water at the rate of five knots per hour. The captain's face brightened once more, for he thought it possible that, as the "Sparta" was a fast sailer, he might keep beyond the reach of the schooner's guns until night, and under its cover make his escape. Not so; thought Edward Duvalle;—he knew the superior qualities of the chase, and as he saw that her last sail was set, and that the wind now favoured her, she would soon be alongside.

"It is useless, Captain Wingate, to attempt to escape her," said Edward, energetically. "Let us prepare to meet her like men."

"You seem to know more of this vessel than one could possibly learn by a few moments look through a spy-glass."

The youth turned to conceal his suddenly suffused cheeks, which this remark caused; but re-assuring himself, he thus replied,—

"I have seen her once before."

"Where?" questioned the captain, eagerly, with suspicion lurking in his countenance.

"In Baltimore," replied Duvalle, promptly.

"Ah! know you her commander?"

"Question me not now, for the love of Heaven, Captain Wingate. You will know all soon! I have sworn to assist you in repelling the ferocious villains! and I will keep the oath! They know that you have a large amount of specie on board, and will make a desperate attempt to obtain it."

The bold and ingenuous manner of the strange youth almost confounded the captain. Still he felt that he could trust him, for he had been a witness of his noble prowess in saving the life of Fanny Floyd.

"Your language fills me with amazement," said he, as he regarded him closely for several moments before speaking.

Before Duvalle could reply, a shot was fired from the schooner, which, however, fell short of the ship; at the same time a black flag, with a dragon emblazoned upon it, was unfurled on board of the piratical craft, as she proved now to be.

"Mr. Duvalle," said the captain, seizing the youth by the hand, "I feel that I can place implicit confidence in you. There is no time to be lost. To what station shall I appoint you?"

"Give me a complement of fearless men, and charge of one of the guns upon the quarter-deck."

"That will be the post of danger."

"Then I have the greater reason for preferring it."

"Do as you will; my first officer shall take charge of the other; while I will give orders to the crew and passengers who are armed with muskets."

Everything was prepared for action without the least confusion. The musketeers were ordered below to await until the pirates should attempt to board the ship. The female passengers, of whom there were several, were entreated to go below, and on no consideration to expose themselves during the impending conflict. With reluctance they left the deck for the lower cabin, which comparatively, was a place of safety from the shot of the enemy.

"Captain Wingate," said Duvalle, in a low tone. "You have a dangerous man among your ship's crew."

"Impossible!" exclaimed the commander, with increased surprise, as his eye sought out each man upon deck. "There is but one on board who has not sailed with me before."

"True, and he is now below."

"You mean Big Tom."

"The same."

"To my knowledge he has shown no symptoms of insubordination?"

"But I repeat, he is a dangerous man; and would, were it in his power, deliver your vessel into the hands of the bloody demons who sail under yon piratical flag."

" You amaze me!"

" Take my advice, and while he is sleeping below, order his arrest, put him in irons, and stow him away in the hold. Be cautious, too, how you approach him ;

he has loaded pistols concealed about his person, and will make a desperate resistance."

Ah !" exclaimed the captain, " a light breaks in upon me. He is in some way c nnected with this craft, and you——"

" Say nought of me !" interrupted Duvalle. " I am bound by a voluntary oath to serve you, and let this day's events corroborate my sincerity."

No. 2.

"I will trust you, and be guided by your advice, whatever your motive may be ; and will immediately order the confinement of Big Tom," said the captain, as he turned upon his heel to put the resolve into immediate execution.

"Stay," said the youth. "I must not be known to him in this business. No good and much harm may result from it."

"Your wish shall be regarded," said the captain, as he left Duvalle, and went forward and called three of his trusty crew into his state-room. Here he made known to them the duty they had to perform, and instructed them on no condition to alarm the crew or passengers upon the deck ; and also gave them to understand that he would be near them in case an emergency should require any assistance from another. He then gave the chief man hand-cuffs and chains, which he first carefully wrapped in a handkerchief that they might be concealed from the crew, as they passed along the deck from the state room to the forecastle.

This precaution, Captain Wingate deemed essential, as he was not a little suspicious that Big Tom might have caused a seditious influence among some of his crew.

The men went forward and entered the forecastle, where Big Tom and his companions were quietly sleeping away their watch below. At the same time the captain had made his way through the piles of freight and luggage which were stowed between decks, and took his place beside a secret panel affording an entrance into the forecastle if desirable.

The heavy report of a gun from the chase at this moment caused Big Tom to start from his berth, when he was immediately seized by the three sailors. But his immense strength proved too great for them. With his athletic arms he threw them from him as if they had been children, and drawing two pistols from beneath his jacket, he stood in an attitude of defence, with one in each hand.

"I'll send the first man to h——ll, who dares approach me," exclaimed he in defiance, and with stentorian voice.

The sailors shrunk from him with fear, for although they knew his immense strength, yet he had never appeared to them so formidable and terrible before. The noise had awakened the other sleepers, who leaped from their berths suddenly, but seemed undecided how to act ; it had also reached the ears of black Pete, who rushed down the forecastle steps, and perceiving Big Tom with pistols levelled, he leaped, with the quickness of a cat upon his back, and seized the barrel of the pistol in the sailor's left hand, which was discharged and the contents lodged in the ceiling above. The heavy stroke of a sabre from an unseen hand caused the other weapon to drop to the floor while his right arm now hung powerlessly by his side. This last blow was struck by the captain, who, perceiving the desperate state of things, slipped the panel noiselessly aside, and thus decided the affray. The powerful sailor made no further resistance, but submitted to his captor's will. They heavily ironed him, and placed him in a secure place in the hold.

CHAPTER III.

THE CLIPPER "VISION" ALIAS "SPITFIRE."—A FRIGATE IS DESCRIED.—CAPTAIN RINGBOLD AND HIS LIEUTENANT, DE SOLO.—THE MUTINOUS PIRATE.—SANGUINARY PUNISHMENT.—RINGBOLD'S PLAN TO CAPTURE THE MERCHANTMAN, AND ESCAPE THE FRIGATE.

THE clipper " Vision " (for this in reality was the name of the chase) was the identical vessel that Captain Wingate had seen in the harbour of the monumental city but two or three weeks previous. She had, since leaving port, been entirely repainted, and a dark strip of canvas nailed upon her stern with the word "Spitfire" painted upon it, now successfully concealed her real name from view. As the captain of the "Sparta" had predicted, she was truly a pirate. He would hardly have suspected her when she first hove in sight, had not the tell-tale top-gallant sail, together with the sudden radical change in her appearance, struck him as not being altogether consistent with the common course of things.

The "Spitfire," as we shall now term the corsair, was one of the finest models of naval architecture of her class then upon the ocean. Her hull fore and aft was of the most graceful symmetry; and her long tapering masts and spars were finely proportioned to the hull. She was about one hundred and seventy tons burthen, and had sailed from Baltimore with fifteen men, but her force had since been augmented to sixty, and they were as fierce a looking set of fellows as ever trod the deck of a corsair. She carried eight brass guns, four on each side, each of six pounds calibre; four small pieces aft, and two long eighteens forward. She had been in pursuit of the "Sparta" for several days, and on the morning when the merchantman was descried from her look-out, her boats were ordered out, and every exertion used to overhaul their intended prize. Their exertions were continued until about ten A.M., when a large vessel hove in sight directly astern, which the captain of the pirate, after gazing at her carefully through a superior telescope, made out to be a large double-banked frigate, but she was too far distant from the corsair captain to enable him to discern to what nation she belonged; and so far distant from the "Sparta" that she had not as yet been descried by that vessel. The pirate captain immediately resolved to retard the speed of his vessel which was now under full sail, until nightfall, when he should be enabled to board the merchantman without being observed by the frigate; and at the same time to keep a respectable and safe distance from the latter craft. This expedient worked successfully, and the three vessels in a line, were now moving through the water at about an equal speed. Consequently, on board of the pirate, there was but little to do, except to keep a good look out for the frigate and to vary the speed of the craft as circumstances required.

On the quarter-deck of the "Spitfire" stood the pirate captain, whose name was Ringbold, conversing with his first lieutenant, a swarthy visaged Spaniard, whom the captain addressed as De Soto. The former was a muscular-looking man of about forty-five years of age, with huge whiskers and shaggy eye-brows; the latter over-arching a pair of twinkling eyes. His complexion was florid, and were it not for a rigid and severe expression which rested upon his countenance, he would have been called by many, a noble looking man. His manners and accent were evidently English; and his bearing was commanding and dignified. His dress was wholly unlike that of a pirate, but nearly resembled the undress uniform of officers of rank in the British navy. His only weapons were a jewelled-hilted rapier which hung by his side, and a small pair of pistols were placed in his belt directly beneath his right arm; while his men carried heavy cutlasses, pistols, and knives.

De Soto, the Spaniard, was richly and elegantly attired; he sported a crimson cap, with plumes fastened in a socket of precious stones; a light gold embroidered tunic, and a waistcoat with various devices elaborately wrought with gold, silver, and other threads. Upon his shirt bosom sparkled a brilliant star, formed of diamonds of immense value. He also wore a diamond-hilted sword, and gold buckles set with emeralds and rubies. His jet black and glossy hair curled in profusion about his neck, which was laid almost bare. His complexion was dark but clear, and when he smiled, displayed a set of teeth of which he might well have been proud, so perfectly regular and white did they appear. He was pleasing and gentlemanly in his manners, and affable in conversation; and he seemed better fitted to grace the drawing rooms of a king's court than the deck of a bloody Corsair. But De Soto was a perfect demon in the hour of battle, but apparently calm and pleasing as a child when the strife was over and the victory won. He was ambitious in the extreme, and more than one unsuccessful attempt had been made to for ever silence Captain Ringbold, that he might become monarch of the fleet then under the orders of his captain, and which were ploughing more than one ocean in search of plunder.   But, fortunately for him, his attempts to supplant his superior had never been discovered, otherwise he long since would have been dangling at the fore-yard arm.

"Haul down the black flag!" shouted the captain, the moment that the frigate was discovered.

"Ay, ay, sir," answered one of the men, who promptly executed the order.

"Captain Ringbold," said the lieutenant, as he came aft, after ordering the gunners to cease firing, "we are in an awkward predicament ; if we run away from the frigate we shall lose the prize that we have been so long in search of."

"The frigate be d——d!" replied the captain.

"She is a match for two or three just like us."

"Where she a match for the d——l himself I would not make an effort to escape until we had transferred the golden treasures of the 'Sparta' to the 'Spitfire.'"

"Then we had better crowd on all canvas and board the ship as speedily as possible," said De Soto.

"When I give orders to that effect, see that they be promptly executed, but I require no dictation or advice," replied Ringbold, with severity.

"But I merely intended to suggest——"

"Your suggestions, Mr. De Soto, are entirely superfluous.   I have my course marked out and shall follow it, though a dozen frigates were after me. The 'Spitfire' is sailing just fast enough."

The lieutenant finding the captain in ill-humour, thought it wise not to oppose him, though he thought he must be insane to allow the craft to sail at no greater speed than the heavy merchantman, after which they had so long been in chase.

The wind was now increasing each moment, and the "Spitfire" evidently began gaining slowly upon the "Sparta."

"Forward there!" shouted the captain.   "Down with the foresail."

"Ay, ay, sir," shouted one of the men, and the order was executed with promptness.

This order not only surprised the lieutenant, but the men forward could not penetrate the design of their chief in taking the very means to place their lives in jeopardy.   Though they felt dissatisfied with the commander's course, they dared not utter a word of complaint so that it might reach his ears.   But when the lieutenant found occasion to go forward he was questioned by the men on deck in regard to Rigbold's singular conduct.

"We shall be blown to h—ll !" exclaimed a ferocious looking sailor, addressing the lieutenant.   "If we allow that black-looking frigate to bring its double-tiered battery to bear upon us, we may reconcile ourselves either to become food for sharks, or dangle in the air with a bit of rigging about our necks."

"That's just what I think," responded another sailor ; "and the sooner we can show the frigate a clean pair of heels the better."

"Captain Ringbold thinks otherwise," remarked De Soto.   "I must confess that I do not like so close an approximation to so formidable an enemy."

"And why do you not tell him so ?" asked one of the men.

"I have done so, and he not only scorned my words but insulted me," replied the lieutenant.

"Then I'll take the responsibility of hoisting this rag up again !" said the sailor who first spoke, when he saw that the captain had gone below.

It required more than the efforts of one to hoist the heavy sail, and there was not another on deck who dared to assist in this mutinous act.   The sailor having great strength succeeded in raising it two thirds up, when Captain Ringbold suddenly appearing on deck, demanded if any of the officers had given orders to the man to hoist the foresail.   On receiving a negative answer he drew from his belt a pistol, a report followed, and the foolish mutineer lay weltering in his blood upon the deck,

"Throw him overboard," ordered Ringbold.   "Such shall be the fate of all who disobey my orders."

The command was promptly obeyed, and order was again restored, though more than one pirate swore, inaudibly, revenge upon their sanguinary commander.

The lieutenant again rejoined Ringbold upon the quarter-deck. The latter now was in better humour since he had had an opportunity of venting his spleen upon the disobedient sailor, and treated his first officer with less sullenness than he had done a few moments before.

"Take a cigar, Mr. de Soto." said Ringbold, as a negro boy came forth from the cabin, and placed a box of fine Havannahs before him.

"With pleasure," replied the lieutenant as he helped himself and took a seat near the captain.

"We shall have a dull day after all," remarked the captain; "but the evening will prove a busy one."

"It will, indeed, if the frigate in pursuit overtakes us," replied De Soto.

"There is but little danger of that so long as we can carry a rag of canvas. We can run her hull down in half an hour."

"Then what possible danger is to be apprehended from overhauling the merchantman, securing our booty, and then showing the frigate a clean pair of heels."

"The danger is this, Mr. de Soto. I am sure that the commander of the merchantman will do all in his power to resist us; at any rate, there will be sufficient delay to enable the frigate to heave in sight of him, if he has not already discovered her. If we should board the 'Sparta' in sight of the man-of-war, the character of our vessel would be instantly known, and we should be dogged by her from one ocean to another."

"May I ask if your plan of attack is fully matured?"

"It is. You will perceive that for the last two hours the frigate has not gained upon us, nor have we gained upon the merchantman, although both are under every rag of canvas that they can carry, while we are walking through the water with equal speed under two-thirds of ours."

"True—I have noticed it."

"Now my intention is to incite the merchantman to press forward as fast as possible, at the same time to show to the frigate that we have no anxiety in regard to her proximity. As soon as it is sufficiently dark, I shall crowd all sail, overhaul the 'Sparta,' obtain her treasures, and when morning dawns be far out of sight."

"Excellent, excellent!" exclaimed de Soto. "I admire your judicious plan; I will never again be alarmed; I confess that I considered your strange movements dangerous, if not foolish."

"Mr. de Soto," resumed Ringbold, "I would, if possible, have the ship captured without the firing of another gun. To effect this, I have an important duty for you to perform."

"I shall feel proud of any appointment whereby I may show my zeal in your service."

"As soon as it is dark, man the cutter and gig with fifteen men each, and pull with all speed for the ship. Be sure that they are well armed. Should you meet with more resistance than you can cope with, display a signal light, and the schooner shall be run alongside with all possible despatch. In all probability, the two guns on the ship's quarter will be found spiked at the time they have most need of them. Drive the passengers and crew into the hold, and fasten down the hatches. Harry Tempest, if he has done his duty faithfully, will disclose to you where the ship's treasures are concealed. Have everything ready to transfer to the 'Spitfire' the moment she ranges alongside."

"Your orders shall be strictly obeyed," replied the lieutenant. "What disposition shall be made of the ladies, if any are found on board?"

"Secure them in the lower cabin; or, rather leave them to the disposal of Harry. He is fond of the fair creatures, and as he has already, without doubt, made himself very agreeable to them, let his humour be indulged."

"I trust their influence over him will not cause him to turn traitor."

"No danger—not the slightest. Although Harry was not cut out for a free rover, yet he has never deceived me, and I would trust him on an enterprise like the present as soon as I would trust myself. He is a noble fellow, and knows no master or sire save me."

" I have heard that there was some mystery connected with his birth, but I never learned the particulars."

" They will all be brought to light in due time. I, alone, possess the great secret —and when I have done with his services his true position in life shall be divulged."

" I have been told that he has refused promotion even under you."

" Yes, uniformly. I have offered him the place you now fill ; and even tried to persuade him to take command of a clipper which I would have procured and equipped for him in the most efficient manner. No, he prefers executing my orders, rather than to take the responsibility of a command himself. He does not lack courage, for he is ever upon deck in the hour of battle, though I never saw him brandish a cutlass or discharge a pistol, except by way of amusement. Yet there is no duty on board of a vessel that he is not fully competent of performing."

" Have you no fears that he will ever prove treacherous to you ?"

" None ; for well he knows that then his hopes of penetrating the mystery which hangs over him would perish for ever. With my own hands would I destroy the last trace which stands between him and an exalted station in society."

" Surely you have him secure enough."

" Yes, and as he has done me good service, I can't help liking the youth, not-withstanding I strongly suspect he despises our roving profession."

It was now five o'clock in the afternoon, and the officers of the " Spitfire " were summoned to the cabin to dinner, leaving the deck in charge of the second lieu-tenant, with proper instructions as to her course, speed, &c.

The merchantman and pirate were within four miles of each other, while the frigate was yet eight or nine miles astern of the schooner. At seven o'clock, Captain Ringbold and his lieutenant again appeared on deck. The latter imme-diately made preparations to execute his commission, and when the pirate crew ascertained that there was a prospect of having something to do, they gave three loud huzzas, and went about their duty with alacrity.

The sun had disappeared, and the shades of evening had veiled the frigate from view, when the captain exclaimed in thundering tones,—

" Haul up the foresail !"

" Set the gaft-topsail !"

" There she walks through it gloriously !" continued Ringbold, as he looked over the side of his trim craft.

In the meantime two of the boats had been lowered from the davits, and thirty picked men, well armed, were ready to push off at a moment's warning.

" All ready ! pull away, my hearties !" exclaimed De Soto, as he leaped into the stern of the gig.

The remainder of the crew on board gave them three hearty cheers, which was returned by the men in the boats. They now plied the oars, and shot ahead of the schooner rapidly, notwithstanding she was under a pretty good headway. In half an hour they had so far distanced the " Spitfire " as to lose sight of her altogether.

CHAPTER IV.

THE CONDUCT OF THE PIRATE ACCOUNTED FOR.—PREPARATION FOR DEFENCE.—THE
BOATS OF THE SCHOONER HEAVE IN SIGHT.—ARE HAILED BY THE CAPTAIN, AND A
MUSKET-BALL RETURNED.—THE FIRST GUN FROM THE "SPARTA,"AND ITS TERRIBLE
EXECUTION.—DISMAY OF THE PIRATES.—A PORTION OF THEM GAIN THE DECK OF
THE "SPARTA."—A DESPERATE CONFLICT.—CONDUCT OF THE STRANGER, DUVALLE.
SINGLE COMBAT, IN WHICH DE SOTO IS DEFEATED BY EDWARD DUVALLE.

IT had been a day of fearful anxiety on board of the "Sparta." The apparent lack
of exertion on the part of the pirate, and the hauling down of the foresail, did not
escape the observation of Captain Wingate, yet he was at a loss to account for the
strange movement.

"The pirate has taken in her foresail," said the captain to Duvalle, as soon as
he had reached the deck, after the arrest of Big Tom. "This looks strange."

"It is unaccountable to me," replied Duvalle, "unless, perchance, they are not
yet fully prepared to attack your ship."

"Or, perhaps, they imagine that we are too strong for them," added the captain.

Duvalle shook his head as he thought how little Captain Wingate knew of the
terrible power contained within that graceful craft.

"It is my opinion," said he at length, "that the pirate chief does not intend to
make the attack until after dark."

"Yes, yes—that's his game, without doubt," responded Wingate, "and I thank
you for giving me an insight into his design. But we'll be on the look-out, and
when the bloody devils do show themselves they'll be sure to be warmly received.
But I must go below and inform the ladies that there is no immediate danger, for
if they find out that I am hencooping them up without a reasonable cause, they'll
be down upon me like a white squall after a calm.

*   *   *   *   *   *   *

It was now evening. The bright constellations were reflected from the deep,
and the noble ship with majestic and graceful motion, was slowly breasting the long
rolling billows. The wind was light and steady, and there was a perfect silence
maintained on the "Sparta's" deck. The captain and first officer, together with
Duvalle, stood on the quarter-deck, their eyes kept to the leeward, and they
carefully listened as if expecting every moment to catch some sounds from the
pursuing vessel, which became utterly imperceptible soon after the sun had sunk
beneath the western wave.

Every man, with the exception of Mr. Floyd, including crew and passengers,
were now upon the deck of the merchantman, and altogether they mustered
thirty-five ; but little more than half the number on board the chase. They had
been harangued by the captain to some effect, and every one uttered a resolve that
they preferred to die fighting manfully, than to be murdered in cool blood, by devils
wearing the semblance of humanity! All of them were armed with muskets,
with the exception of a small detachment to man the guns. Each one was ordered
to preserve the utmost silence until the captain's orders were heard. Thus were
the entire resources of the ship judiciously arranged, and the men put under proper
instructions. It is true they had but little hope of repelling the piratical crew, yet
they vowed to sell their lives dearly.

"Hark!" exclaimed Duvalle to the captain ; "I hear the sound of oars!"

In another moment, clapping his night glass to his eye, he continued, "I perceive two boats, fully manned, rowing with all their might towards us."

"Sure enough," said the captain ; "the devils will be under our heels in fifteen
minutes. How many do you make out their number to be?"

"Not upwards of thirty," replied Duvalle.

"Not more than thirty?" reiterated Wingate ; "our number exceeds that."

"You must consider that they are all fighting men."

"But have we not the advantage of them?" asked the captain, regaining confidence. "Pooh! they mistake our strength. We can send half of them to Davy Jones, before one can gain a footing upon the 'Sparta's' deck. I really like the shape they come in, and quite relish the little brush that is about to come off."

Saying this the animated captain went along the deck to raise the hopes and spirits of the men.

"Cheer up, my hearties!" said he; "they are coming in gig loads, instead of administering doses of hot shot from their long eighteens, into the ribs of the old 'Sparta.' How I should glory in capturing this schooner. It would be a good joke to tell of when we got into port—how an old merchantman, with a handful of men and passengers, captured a fast-sailing piratical craft, heavily manned and armed. Keep cool, my lads, when the boats come within musket shot. Fire not a gun until you hear the word of command, and then take sure aim and blaze away."

The boats could now be discerned with the naked eye. Captain Wingate took his station on the quarter-deck, and through his speaking trumpet, vociferated aloud.

"Boat ahoy!"

No answer was returned, but the men plied their oars more briskly than before.

"Boat ahoy!" again shouted the captain.

A flash and a sharp musket report was heard, and an ounce ball pierced a hole through the speaking trumpet which Captain Wingate held in his hand.

"The devils are sharp shooters!" exclaimed he to Duvalle, as the ball whistled through his instrument.

"Shall I give them a salute from this six pounder?" asked Duvalle.

"Wait until you cannot fail of your mark?"

"In a minute more they will be so near us, that it will be impossible to depress the piece sufficiently to bear upon them."

"Take a good aim and let them have it! Mind the heave of the sea."

"Stand by, my boys!" exclaimed Duvalle, while he directed the piece. "All ready! Fire!"

The match was applied—the sea for a moment was illuminated, and amid the booming of the canon—a crash was heard!—and shrieks and oaths from dying men fell upon the ears of those upon the "Sparta's" deck!

The smoke cleared away, the roar of the gun echoed feebly in the distance, and with it were hushed the groans and curses of the wounded and dying! The foremost boat was crushed, and no less than ten men had found a watery grave! Those who miraculously escaped were picked up by the lagging boat, which retarded her progress but for a moment. De Soto, the lieutenant, was on board this boat, and when he saw the fate of so many of his brave men, it only increased his desperation, and muttering awful curses and damnable oaths, he ordered his men to fire a volley upon the quarter deck of the ship, and then to pull heartily and board her, where they would have an opportunity amply to revenge the fate of their fallen comrades!

"Can't you give them another dose!" said Wingate, as he saw the effect of Duvalle's well-directed fire, and just as the shot of the pirates pattered like hail stones about them.

"No—they will be under our stern in one moment," answered Edward. "Now's the time for the musketeers!"

The men were all ordered on the quarter-deck, with their guns cocked and primed, awaiting the word of command.

"Ready! Aim! Fire!" ordered the first mate, who now acted as captain of the raw marines.

"Bravo! Bravo!" exclaimed the captain, as he saw three or four of the men fall.

The muskets were again loaded, and another volley was poured upon them, but the execution was not so great as at the first fire, the pirates being now nearly under the stern of the ship. In a moment more they began clambering up the ship's sides but many were beaten into the water with the butts of the muskets, and but few gained a footing upon the deck. These fought with the fury of madmen, and made siderable slaughter among the ship's crew! De Soto and three or four others had gained the quarter deck by means of the davits tackle, and here a most desperate combat ensued. Duvalle had shot the first that gained a footing, and disarmed him of a heavy cutlass with which he kept the others at bay. Captain Wingate, with one or two others, rushed to his assistance, and succeeded in engaging and beating down, with such weapons as they could find, all but the leader, who was in the meantime in deadly combat with Duvalle.

"Traitor!" exclaimed the enraged pirate lieutenant. "Thy hour is come."

"Pirate! murderer! merciless wretch!" returned Duvalle, in thundering tones. "This moment is worth living a whole life for. God be praised that he has spared thy miserable life thus far through this scene of carnage, that I may perform one good deed ere I die!"

No. 3.

" Prate no more, vile traitor. Think not, because we are partially defeated through your damnable treachery, you or this ship's crew are safe. Ere midnight, every one of you will be weltering in your gore."

" If my arm fails to let out your savage blood, think not to escape."

" Shall I blow his brains out?" ejaculated Captain Wingate, after the strife was quelled on the other parts of the deck.

" No; he must die by my hands. Let no one interfere. He is the pirate De Soto, second in command to the devil, Ringbold."

" And what art thou, then," questioned De 'Soto, " but the devil's own son ?"'

" Ringbold is not my father, and thou knowest it, villain."

" Then thou'rt worse—an illegitimate foundling, picked up upon the sea, where thou hadst been cast by thy unnatural mother."

" Liar ! I'll hear no more."

Their blades crossed. Both looked on each other with the ferocity of tigers. It was an anxious moment. The lieutenant was evidently Duvalle's superior in strength, but the latter could boast of greater skill in handling the cutlass. Blow after blow was struck, but not a drop of blood was yet drawn. Owing to some blood upon the deck, Duvalle slipped as he was parrying a blow, and his weapon was knocked from his hands. De Soto was about to cut him down, when, in an instant, the weapon was restored to him, and in time to enable him to ward off the powerful stroke which the pirate aimed at his head. Duvalle regained his feet, and renewed the fight with more eagerness than before. It was for some time doubtful how the contest would end. They seemed evenly matched. But Captain Wingate watched every movement with the eagerness of a cat, resolving if Duvalle again laboured under a disadvantage, to blow out the pirate's brains at once. This, however, was not destined to be the result. De Soto's power began to fail him, and his antagonist, acting with greater coolness, began now to press him hard, and seizing an opportunity, by a dextrous movement of his arm, the cutlass flew from the pirate's hand. In another moment his headless trunk lay weltering in purple gore !

" Bravo ! huzza ! huzza !" shouted Captain Wingate, and a hearty response was heard from all on board.

The decks were now cleared from the dead bodies of the pirates, and thrown overboard. One of the foremast-men of the ship's crew was found among the slaughtered. This loss, with two or three others who were slightly wounded, was all that the ship's crew sustained in this well-fought but desperate contest.

The ladies, having been informed that the pirates were defeated, came upon deck, and witnessed the single combat between Duvalle and De Soto. It was none other than Fanny Floyd who picked up Edward's sabre when he was by accident disarmed, and quickly placed it in his right hand. The captain was a witness of the heroic act, and applauded her openly for it, and afterwards informed Duvalle the circumstance.

" Your gallant deeds and noble bearing during our desperate conflict with the bloody devils, deserve more than our warmest thanks," said Captain Wingate to his heroic passenger. " I hope yet to have an opportunity to manifest it oy a more substantial token."

" I have done but my duty, sir."

" The honour of the victory we have achieved belongs solely to you."

" Remember, the victory is not yet won."

" I do not think one has escaped to tell of their defeat."

" True, sir ; yet, notwithstanding we have killed a score or two of the merciless buccaniers, there are enough left on board of the corsair to man every gun that she carries ; and with one or two broadsides, she might easily sink your ship."

" Perhaps they will send another detachment to look after their comrades. If they do, they must share a like fate."

" They will not do that," replied Duvalle ; " it is my opinion that we shall not see the schooner again before midnight, though I should recommend the strictest look-out to be kept, and that the men be prepared at a moment's warning. It is customary on board of the corsair, when boats are sent on any expedition in the night, to carry with them a signal-light to display if they need further assistance from the vessel. Here is a lantern which one of your men has taken from the pirate's gig, now alongside, which confirms me in my belief that it was brought with them for this very purpose. If no signal is discovered by the corsair captain, he will, of course, presume that the ship is captured and now in the possession of his crew."

"That being the case, what's best to be done?" asked Captain Wingate, musingly.

"We cannot escape her nor capture her, unless by a *ruse*," replied Duvalle "but it will prove a desperate and bloody one."

"So much the greater glory," answered the captain, with enthusiasm. "This is the first time I ever did any fighting in my life, and now that I have got a taste of it, and had an opportunity to prove to myself whether I am a coward or not, I could enjoy a battle with these sea-robbers every morning by way of getting up an appetite for breakfast."

"Then, be assured, if we engage these fellows again, you will require more than a double allowance, to-morrow morning," replied Edward, facetiously.

"Come, let's hear your plan for a *ruse*, and I'll follow it. Although I'm monarch of this deck, yet under the circumstances I'm willing to listen to your direction or dictation."

"In the first place, I propose that the clothes which were stripped from the bodies of the slain pirates be distributed among your men, with orders to disguise themselves therewith immediately, so far as they will go. Let the disguised men be stationed near the gangway, and order all the others below until a signal is given for them to reappear upon the deck."

"Excellent, I see it all!" interrupted the captain, rapturously.

"Then back the main topsail, and bring your ship to——"

"What? and allow the devils to board us at once?" ejaculated the commander, somewhat staggered at this latter suggestion.

"It is your only course to save the vessel and your lives."

"Then our chance is indeed a small one."

"Not so. You have not heard my whole plan."

"Well, go on. I'll listen with all my ears."

"With De Soto's wardrobe, I intend to disguise myself, and by calling into aid a little imitative talent that I fortunately possess, I shall be enabled to personate him whom I have just slain, with tolerable accuracy; at any rate, sufficiently so to deceive the corsair chief. When the schooner heaves in sight, I will hail her and tell him that he had better not run her alongside, as there is danger from an explosion, giving him to understand that there is fire in the hold, but to send another boat, with a full complement of men to assist us in putting out the fire and getting the treasures upon deck. Should the pirate chief put off in the boat for the ship, by all means let him be taken alive; I have an account to adjust with him ere he dies. On no consideration let a gun be fired, but silence the pirates with swords and cutlasses; otherwise the report of muskets would alarm the schooner, and we should be fired upon at once. Have no lights burning about the ship, that our proceedings be not discovered by those left on board of the corsair. Should we succeed in this, I will again hail her to come alongside, as no further danger may be apprehended from the pretended fire. The moment that she comes up, and with her grappling-irons is made fast to the ship, let that be a signal to board her at once. Station half your force at the gangway for defence, and I will lead the other half on board of the pirate from the ship's quarter-deck. In ten minutes after that, our fates and the contest will be decided."

"Bravo, bravo! give us your hand. You're the boy for me!" exclaimed the captain in raptures. "You deserve to be the admiral of a whole fleet. If I ever step my foot on *terra firma* again, I'll see that your name shall go down to posterity with the best of 'em. You shall be immortalised, if brave deeds can give a man immortality."

"Thank you, captain, but I have no ambition for such distinction," replied Edward. "On defeating the pirates and taking their chief alive, depend all my hopes for the future; and since I find that you have good and brave men on board of your ship, there is a possibility of your becoming the victors. Your chance is more than equal if I can deceive them by my *ruse*. But, Captain Wingate, before we again go to our duty, I have one request to make."

"Had you a thousand to make they should be granted, my friend."

"Should I fall in the contest, I wish not to leave an ignominious name behind me. It is true, I never harmed the least of God's creation, except in defence ; yet should I die without penetrating the awful mystery which keeps me from a knowledge of myself, a bloody pirate's name would live after me !"

"A pirate ! You a pirate ! I'll never believe it."

"And yet more than half of my life has been spent in the company of pirates, in their haunts upon the land, and in their vessels on the sea ; but for all this I deserve not this murderous appellation."

"I believe it—every word you utter."

"Now, should it be my fate to fall, you will find among my papers a detailed account of my own life and actions, since I was a child, much of it, indeed, written from memory, but nevertheless correct in each particular. Give this little history to the one whose address it bears."

"Your request shall be faithfully attended to, should you possibly meet the fate you apprehend," replied the captain. "May God spare your life, and bring you many days of happiness and comfort."

"Should Ringbold fall, I claim his person and private papers," resumed Edward. "For in his possession the secret of my birth is carefully kept. He has often asserted in my hearing, that when he falls,—should I prove treacherous to him,—for ever dies the mystery. On this account I would have him taken alive."

"Cheer up, my young friend," said the captain, as he observed that Edward looked despondingly. "I feel that upon you the lives of all on board of this ship depend."

"Then, may Heaven assist me, and nerve my arm for the impending conflict."

Saying which, Edward and the captain went about their duty ; the former to prepare for the ruse he intended to play upon their sanguinary foe, and the latter to rouse the ardour of the passengers and the ship's crew.

CHAPTER V.

HAILING THE SCHOONER.—GLEE OF THE PIRATES AT THEIR GOLDEN PROSPECTS.—SUCCESS OF THE RUSE.—CONSTERNATION AND DESTRUCTION OF THE SECOND DETACHMENT OF PIRATES.—DUVALLE AND FIFTEEN MEN PREPARE TO EMBARK IN THE BOATS FOR THE PURPOSE OF ATTACKING THE "SPITFIRE."

It was about midnight, as Duvaile had predicted, when the "Spitfire" hove in sight. She was yet a mile and a half distant, but could be distinctly discerned through a night-glass. Captain Wingate, with great coolness and intrepidity, gave orders to take in all the small sails, heave the ship to, and await the coming up of their fearful enemy. All the instructions and suggestions of the young and active passenger were implicitly followed ; the men then upon deck wearing the garb of the pirates that were killed in the first conflict, and Duvalle fully equipped with the arms and gay attire of the corsair lieutenant ; while the remainder of the crew and passengers were waiting below with beating hearts the summons to the bloody battle in anticipation. Not many minutes after the ship was hove to, the "Spitfire" had come within hailing distance, when Duvalle mounted the traffrail of the ship, with the captain's speaking trumpet, and with a loud but assumed voice, hailed,—

"Schooner, ahoy!"

"Hilloa!" was the response a moment or two afterwards. "What ship is that?"

"The Sparta! Lieutenant De Soto! of and from Baltimore, bound to Rio Janeiro, with a rich cargo. What schooner is that?"

"The Spitfire! Captain Ringbold! on a cruise. Shall we run alongside?"

"No!" replied the assumed De Soto. "Send a boat, we need another to remove the specie! Besides the ship is on fire and there is no time to lose!"

"Ay, ay!" returned the corsair chief.

All was now animation and glee on board of the "Spitfire." The crew shouted and danced for joy at the golden prospects before them. Their supposed prize they had watched and dogged for several weeks, and to obtain so easy a victory was a matter of congratulation, particularly to several novices in the profession, which had been enlisted since the schooner left Baltimore.

"Comrades!" exclaimed the pirate chief, rubbing his hands with exultation. "Launch the long boat, and pull for the ship with all despatch! The prize is ours—and a golden one she'll prove to us. De Soto has done up the business bravely! Work briskly, my lads! bear a hand, every one of you!"

"Ay, ay, sir!" shouted all the crew; and in a few moments the heavy long boat was afloat.

Twenty men were despatched in this boat under the command of the third officer; the captain and ten men remaining in charge of the schooner.

The exulting shouts of the pirate crew reached the ears even of those on board of the ship. But instead of having a disheartening effect, it emboldened their hearts and nerved their arms for the fight. The captain and Duvalle for a few moments awaited with fearful anxiety the success of their project; but when they heard the loud "heave-oh!" of the pirates, the latter knew that they were getting out the long-boat for the purpose of coming on board to assist in removing the treasures of the ship, and therefore, thus far the trick had proved successful.

"It is my opinion, Captain Wingate," remarked our hero, "that this boat's crew can be captured without the firing of a gun!"

"Without the firing of a gun!" ejaculated the commander. "Impossible!"

"It is quite possible, sir," continued Duvalle.

"How so?"

"They come as victors for the spoils which they suppose already theirs. And therefore it is my opinion, they will leave at least their fire-arms behind them!"

"True! you're right. We'll spoil the devils!"

"If they can be destroyed or taken without the firing of cannon or musket, our efforts will be crowned with success," continued Duvalle. "Should firing be heard by the pirate chief, he will suspect that all is not right, and before we know it, he will be pouring his grape and canister into us. Even with half a dozen men he might blow the ship into atoms! On the other hand, by capturing or destroying them with cutlasses and swords, their fate will not be known to Ringbold until it be too late to revenge the slaughter of the crew. As soon as this can be accomplished with as many men as can be spared from the ship we can man three boats, run alongside of the schooner, and before we are suspected, gain possession of her deck, where I hope not only to avenge the wrongs I have done, but to discover the secret of my birth, now only known to the pirate chief!"

"Your plan is all important, I perceive," replied Captain Wingate, "and I will forthwith enforce upon the minds of the men, the necessity of achieving our next victory by the sword alone. If they are not armed with muskets, we can silence half of them while clambering up the ship's side; and then we must be poor, weak soldiers, indeed, if we can't conquer the rest in the same way. But we have no time to talk! There they come, exulting fiercely over their suppose d prize !"

"Sure enough, and they will be under our stern in five minutes."

"Remember, my dear friend," resumed the captain, "if we capture the pirate, you shall have the command, and the largest share of the prize money."

"I want neither," replied Duvalle, "but I shall deem it a special favour if you will allow me to lead those who will be despatched to capture the schooner !"

"By all means; you're just the man! I wouldn't trust another on board the 'Sparta.' I wouldn't trust myself, though from this day henceforth I shall consider myself a fighting man, lacking neither courage nor strength."

After this laudatory remark of the captain, spoken half seriously, and half jokingly, he went among the men on deck, and stationed most of them near the gangway with cutlasses, swords, handspikes and such other weapons as the ship afforded, with the exception of fire-arms, which were removed to a convenient place in case they should be required.

The long-boat of the "Spitfire" was now within a half cable's length distance, when Duvalle (dressed as De Soto) mounted the gangway ladder, where he could be seen by the pirates. They gave him three loud and hearty cheers. He, in return, waved his hat in acknowledgment, and returned to the station he had chosen upon the deck.

"Everything favours our cause," said he in a low voice to those around him. "It appears that they have brought no weapons except their side-arms with them. Wait comrades till the signal for attack is given. Strike not a blow until half-a-dozen at least have reached the deck, and as many more are upon the gangway ladder."

All resolved to adhere closely to Duvalle's instructions, and for a few moments, the utmost silence reigned upon the "Sparta's" decks. The long-boat came thumping against the ship's side; the pirates, impatient and eager to be on the deck of their supposed prize, crowded up the gangway steps in confusion, while many clambered up the ship's side clinging to whatever they could find. In this way eight or ten reached the merchant-man's deck at once; and among them was the second lieutenant of the "Spitfire," who, first perceiving him whom he supposed to be De Soto, ran towards him to congratulate him with extended hand. Instead of taking it, he gave him such a blow with his heavy sabre as nearly to sever his head from his body, and the pirate officer's dead body rolled upon the deck.

So quick was this done, that the pirates, not yet comprehending the snare that had been so ingeniously set for them, looked on the dead body with wonder and amazement! The first impression which thwarted across their minds, was that De Soto had taken this opportunity to avenge himself for some injury that his fellow officer had done him. But a precious few moments did they have to investigate what appeared to them such a profound mystery !

"Now's the time !" shouted Duvalle, in tones of thunder.

"At 'em, my boys !" added Captain Wingate. "Down with the villains! Show no quarter but to those who fall upon their knees and beg for it."

Eight or ten had already fallen by the effectual onslaught made by the crew and passengers, before any began to comprehend the fatal situation in which they found themselves. It was now too late for a retreat. Every man had been brought into the snare, and to fight was all that could be done. Should they sue for mercy on board the ship and obtain it, well they knew that on shore that quality would never be shown to pirates, whose bloody deeds had already chilled the hearts of a multitude. With a desperation and fury, amounting to madness, they drew their cutlasses, and rushed upon their foe. One of the number, recognising Duvalle in De Soto's attire, exclaimed aloud,—

"Ah! we have been betrayed by Harry Tempest, the captain's son!" and singling out Duvalle, he strove with all his might to cut him down, but the pirate found more than his match—at the third blow his skull was split in twain. Those who had been waiting below for further orders, were now summoned to the combat. Seeing a large body of men rushing upon deck, the pirates were dismayed and disheartened. They fell back before their new antagonists. Several tried to jump overboard, but all who attempted it received a blow which sent them to their last account. So well had everything been contrived to meet every possible emergency, that Duvalle had stationed several men along the ship's sides, to prevent any one's escaping alive to give the alarm to those left on board of the schooner.

The pirates fought with a desperation and fury unparalleled. They did not ask for quarter. They did not expect it. But so long as they had life in their bodies, they continued to make resistance. At length, the last one of all those that had left the "Spitfire" in such high glee, was run through the body with a two-edged sword, and fell upon the deck with curses in his mouth.

The "Sparta's" crew had fought nobly their second contest, but five of them were lying among the slaughtered, and several received severe, but not mortal wounds, and were immediately taken below.

Captain Wingate also received a deep sabre cut upon the left arm, but he would not be persuaded to leave the deck, "so long" to use his own expression "as there was a live pirate upon it."

" Your plan thus far has succeeded to admiration," said the captain to Duvalle, as soon as the conflict was over.

" You are severely wounded, Captain Wingate," remarked our hero, as he saw blood gushing out of the sleeve of his coat. " You had better go below and get it dressed."

" There is more important business first to be attended to. In the first place, among the dead bodies upon our deck, are several of our own brave men,—they must be separated. I can't bear the thought of leaving them lying promiscuously together. No—the pirates must be thrown overboard, and our brave but fallen heroes must have Cristian burial."

" In the meantime, captain, shall we board the schooner? Delay is dangerous."

" Yes, my brave friend, and to you shall all the honours of these successive victories be ascribed," replied the captain. " Run up alongside as soon as you have conquered her. I want to see what that craft is made of."

" But should I fail, captain?"

" Fail? Hang me if I believe you would fail if she were a hundred-and-ten gun ship!"

" I think the chances are now decidedly in our favour, but I must have a picked crew."

" Take whom you please, and be sure you select sufficient number."

" Thank you; I have observed who are the best fighting men of all this ship's company, and I can easily make a selection. Fifteen are all that I require. Should I meet with more powerful resistance than I anticipate, a single lantern shall be lighted by one whom I will leave in one of the boats for the purpose. You can then despatch me as many more as you can spare, leaving a sufficient number to man your guns, for in them lay your only hope if this expedition fail."

The captain promising to comply, Duvalle went forward to select his men, leaving it, however, to the choice of each one not to go unless they wished it. Fortunately among the fifteen chosen there was not one who did not feel honored at the distinction. They all attired themselves in garments of the pirates and quickly manned their boats, ready for any order from their heroic leader. Duvalle went aft, and took the captain's hand.

" Farewell!" said he, " for the present! If we ever meet again in this world, it will be this night. Within this hour will be decided my fate, my hopes, happiness, ay, even life itself."

" God be with you, and protect you!" said Captain Wingate, as the tears moistened his eye.

" Everything is prepared; and everything seems to favour our enterprise. The men are getting impatient. Again—farewell!"

" Farewell!" responded the captain, as our hero left him and jumped into the boat which was to take the lead. It was ordered that as they neared the schooner each boat's crew should contrive to board her simultaneously and all rush to the quarter-deck, and secure its possession, where they were to await further orders. They were more than once cautioned not to take the life of the pirate chief, but to take him prisoner and confine him securely beneath the hatches.

CHAPTER VII.

EMBARKATIÓN OF THE " SPARTA'S" CREW UNDER DUVALLE.—THEY BOARD THE " SPITFIRE."—CONFUSION OF THE PIRATES.—A DESPERATE ENCOUNTER BETWEEN OUR HERO AND THE BUCCANEER CHIEF.—THE LATTER IS DEFEATED, AND MADE A PRISONER.—A PART OF THE MYSTERY IS UNRAVELLED.—THE PRIZE ARRIVES ALONGSIDE OF THE SHIP.—JOY OF THE VICTORS.

THE boats being now fully prepared, pushed off from the ship, and as silently as possible the men rowed leisurely for the schooner; as they had been instructed not to waste their strength in making useless haste. As they neared the pirate, Duvalle began singing a buccanier's song, a favourite one of De Soto's, and which the latter often sung for the edification of Ringbold. So perfectly did he imitate the defunct lieutenant, that the pirate chief, who was watching the approach of the boats from the taffrail, did not for a moment suspect that it proceeded from any other than De Soto.

Without the least confusion, and with apparent moderation, the three boats ranged alongside of the schooner; and although the jolly boat Ringbold noticed did not resemble any that belonged to the " Spitfire," yet he thought nothing of it, since he was so fully persuaded in his own mind that the " Sparta" was really his prize. He was just giving orders to his men to assist in taking the treasures on board (for his eye had a moment before, discovered several boxes and casks in each one of the boats, which had been purposely put there to make the deception the more complete), when the boarders almost simultaneously gained the schooner's deck. Some half dozen of the pirates who were to execute the captain's orders in regard to the specie, met their foe face to face, and recognising strangers instead of their own comrades, started back in dread alarm; but before they could gain a defensive position, they were most of them struck down by the quick movements of the boarders.

" To the quarter deck !" exclaimed Duvalle, who saw Ringbold standing in an attitude of amazement, with one or two of the pirates beside him, equally amazed. As some dozen of the boarders rushed towards him, the pirate chief drew his pistols from his belt, and presenting them, commanded in bold authoritative tones,—

"Stand! approach me not ! the first who disobeys dies!"

There was a halt.

" What means this sudden mutiny ? You are mad ! De Soto, speak?" demanded Ringbold.

" Fear not the bloody monster !" eclaimed Duvalle, as, with sword in hand, he rushed towards him, followed by his men who only waited to hear his commands.

Ringbold levelled one of his pistols, but fortunately for Duvalle, it missed fire ; he raised the other, but ere he could pull the trigger it was knocked from his hand by our hero's sword.

" Stand back, my mene," exclaimed he, as several came to his assistance. " He is my prize. Make sure of all the rest of the bloody villains on board, and for this one I'll be accountable!"

" Traitor," exclaimed Ringbold as he now for the first time recognized his captor; and drawing his two edged-sword, he attempted to make a defence, but by a heavy blow from Duvalle's cutlass his sword-arm fell powerless by his side.

"Now, merciless monster, I have thee! It is now my turn to triumph!"

"You have triumphed by treachery most foul."

"Yes, and saved a noble ship's crew from being massacred by your hell-hounds Thank God they have all met with a severe retribution."

"All! did you say?"

"Ay, all but thee; the last and the worst!"

"Do I deserve all this from thy hands, Harry Tempest?"

"Ay, and much more wilt thou receive. Have you not denied me a father; a mother; a brother; a sister? Have you not endeavoured to train me to a life of bloody deeds? Have you not sent me on missions of treachery, far greater than this, which I consider the best, the noblest act of my life? Have you not given out that I am your son?"

No. 4.

"Is that a crime?"

"Yes, in my view the greatest of crimes! Now, Ringbold, Tempest, Burke, or whatever your name may be, give me up all that appertains to the secret of my birth."

"Spare my life;" said the pirate chief, sinking upon his knees, "and you shall know all."

"I will answer for myself and for those under my command. Farther than this I cannot promise you."

"Enough! lead me to my cabin, where the secret shall be disclosed, and the proofs placed in your possession."

Duvalle, knowing the danger of allowing Ringbold the use of his limbs, ordered him to be pinioned and conveyed to the cabin. He submitted to the execution of these orders without a murmur.

The victory on board of the schooner was complete, and she was now nearing the "Sparta" under a light breeze. Meanwhile our hero and the pirate chief were below continuing the conversation which was begun on deck.

"I have always been told by you that I was found at sea," resumed Duvalle.

"And such is the fact."

"What were the circumstances?"

"Be patient, and I will narrate the particulars so far as my memory serves me. I was then a young man of thirty years of age, first lieutenant of a corsair brigantine. We had been chasing for a number of days a Spanish galleon, belonging to Havana, which was bound to Cadiz, with a large amount of specie on board. In the early part of the night we overhauled the galleon and succeeded in boarding her, after a desperate resistance, in which our chief received a mortal wound, and I was immediately, by acclamation, promoted to the command. I had not been long enough in the roving profession to acquire a decided taste for blood; and when I saw, as in this instance, men and women upon their knees, crying for mercy, and at the same time our merciless crew singling them out, and literally hacking them to pieces, my heart sickened within me, and I commanded them to desist from their bloody work. Among those who were saved by the little spark of mercy which then inhabited my soul, were a noble Spanish gentleman about the same age as myself, and his wife, a beautiful young lady, not more than twenty years of age. Notwithstanding I promised that their lives should be spared, they seemed more grieved than before. The lady was indeed frantic with grief, and all my efforts were exhausted in endeavouring to calm her. On inquiring the cause of her singular conduct, I learned that but a few moments before I ordered that their lives should be spared, they had committed to the mercy of the wind and the waves, a little boy not more than two years old! He was placed in an open box, wrapped carefully in blankets, and lowered out of the cabin windows by his parents, who preferred thus to sacrifice their darling child, rather than to see him hacked to pieces before their eyes by piratical savages, as they termed us.

"As we now wished to remove the treasures of the galleon to the brigantine, and to destroy the other by scuttling, I gave notice to the few remaining passengers whom I had spared, that they must quit the vessel, and offered them the galleon's long boat, with provisions and water for five days. This proposition was eagerly embraced, and ere half an hour more had elapsed they cast off from their captured vessel, which went down soon after they and our own crew had left it.

"When morning dawned the long-boat was out of sight, but one of our men espied a box floating upon the waves, which he thought looked very peculiar. On taking my glass and looking at it for a few moments, I saw distinctly the head of a child. I gave orders to lower the jolly-boat, and despatched four of my crew to pick it up, not doubting that it was the child who was set afloat on the night previous from the captured galleon.

"My conjectures were correct. In half an hour the boat returned, bringing back with them a bright and rosy-cheeked boy, together with the box in which he had been so miraculously preserved. The boy, indeed, smiled and prattled as if nothing had happened, until an hour or two had passed, when he began to cry for his mother. I easily appeased his grief by placing within his reach many curiosities which I had gathered in various parts of the world. In a few days he had quite forgotten his parents, and I resolved to adopt him as my own, and called him Harry Tempest, a *nomme de guerre* by which I was then known to the brigantine's crew.

"Among the contents of the box, which had been carefully supplied with pillows, clothes, &c., for the comfort of the little lone mariner, I found a bag of gold, a casket of precious stones, together with sundry other articles of no inconsiderable value. I also found a scrap of paper within the casket, wnich I have ever carried carefully concealed in my bosom!"

"And is it there now?" interrupted Edward Duvalle, eagerly.

"It is," answered the pirate, as with his left hand he drew from his bosom, a small greasy black wallet, made of calfskin. "I have always kept it in this," he continued, handing him the wallet, "and you will find it there now."

With trembling hands Edward opened the wallet, and took therefrom a slip of paper written in the Spanish language, it being the only article it contained, and translated into English, read as follows :—

"At Sea—on board the Spanish Galleon,
San Germano, *July* 10, 1805.

"Holy mother of God! protect the innocent child whom we now consign to the mercy of the winds and the waves. The Galleon has been attacked by pirates, and already they have commenced butchering the passengers and crew. Our hour is near at hand! Should, perchance, the child be living when picked up, rear him as the means accompanying will allow. Should he be dead, give him Christian burial, and may Heaven bless thee for it. Oh, Heaven, who can describe our agony in this, our last but deliberate act."

(Signed,) " Eustaquio San Malo,
" Constanza San Malo."

" The child herein mentioned, you would have me believe——"

" Is yourself," interrupted the pirate.

" Are my father and mother yet living?"

" Of that I cannot inform you. Whether the long boat in which they embarked, ever reached land, I never could ascertain, although I have made frequent inquries."

" What proof have I that you are not even now deceiving me?"

" In that iron chest," answered Ringbold, which you have so often seen it contains, besides a mine of wealth, the identical casket of jewels and the bag of gold."

" Even with this evidence I may be deceived?"

" You will also find in the chest a package of papers, which fortunately fell into my hands, when the passengers' luggage, was overhauled. Among the papers are the marriage certificate of the persons whose names are appended to the slip of paper which you have just read, a register of their boy's birth, and a passport signed by the authorities of Cadiz. Here are the keys," continued the pirate; " I have considered the chest and the wealth it contains my private property; I now transfer it all to you."

" I shall receive nothing from your hands, except that which rightfully belongs to me," replied Duvalle, proceeding to unlock the chest.

He was somewhat astounded on opening it, to behold the vast amount of ill-gotten wealth it contained. By direction of Ringbold, he easily found the package of documents, the casket of jewels and the bag of gold, which he declared rightfully belonged to our hero; and upon perusing the papers, he found that they corroborated the assertions of the pirate.

It was now morning; the schooner, which for the last fifteen minutes had been bearing down for the ship, had now arrived alongside.

Duvalle concealed the papers and casket in his bosom carefully, and placing the pirate chief under the charge of a guard, hastened upon the deck. He was first met by Captain Wingate, who first leaped from his own vessel as she came alongside, while the crew and passengers at the same time gave three hearty cheers.

"Huzza! huzza! my brave boys; you have conquered?" exclaimed the captain of the merchantman, as he embraced the youth. "In the presence of all here assembled, I hereby declare that the three successive victories we have achieved over the pirates, were accompiished through the bravery of this youthful stranger who stands before you."

The air again resounded with cheers; and the ladies who stood upon the quarter-deck of the "Sparta" waved their handkerchiefs in token of their gratitude.

"To him, then, are we indebted for our lives, and our property!"

"No," answered Edward, falling upon his knees, and stretching forth his hands. "To God alone should we render thanks, for guiding us safely through the perils of this night."

They all fell upon their knees and a silent prayer was offered from every heart.

Duvalle now went on board of the ship, and each one of the crew and passengers took him by the hand, and spoke their gratitude. Mr. Floyd, supported by his daughter, came tottering towards him. Edward perceiving them, advanced a step or two, to meet them, when the old man, in fervent language, gave him his blessing. Fanny, beautiful as the morning, stood trembling and blushing by her father's side—she could not speak; but extended her delicate hand, which he took and pressed warmly to his lips. Who can describe the sensations which at that moment agitated her bosom? The youth whom she so fondly loved, and who had so recently caused her to shed bitter tears, in consequence of his parting words, again stood before her with an unclouded brow and a look of hope beaming from his dark eyes. She understood the meaning of his ardent gaze—she recollected his ominous words at their last interview—the mystery of which he spoke—the "dreadful alliance" at which he had hinted; and which she had but vaguely comprehended. She believed that the time had now come when he would no longer condemn himself; and that the events of the last night, in which he had been the chief actor, were but the fulfilment of that at which he had hinted.

"I did not believe, Miss Floyd," said Edward, "that I could again meet thee with pleasure. But the mysterious veil which kept me from a knowledge of myself, I thank Heaven, is no longer before my eyes. I owe this disenthralment from a life of misery to the victory we have achieved; and should we again have an opportunity to confer alone, I will give you an account of my eventful history, including my recent discoveries. But I have a great duty yet to perform. I must seek out my father and mother, if they are in the land of the living. If dead, I will seek out the tombstone which covers their mortal remains, that I may kneel in affliction before it."

Mr. Floyd, hearing the frankly spoken words of our hero, and thinking that perhaps his presence might not be agreeable to the lovers, he gave his arm to one of his black attendants, and tottered towards the companion-way.

"Oh, Edward," replied the blushing girl, looking into his manly countenance; "I thought that we should never meet again, and yet one spark of hope dwelt with me. Say, shall I not now see thee often?"

"Not on board of this ship. Captain Wingate will give me the command of the prize, and I must carry her safely into port. My next duty will be to travel in search of my parents. Should success crown my efforts, but few months will elapse before I shall meet thee again. Should I fail after one year's diligent search, then Fanny, will I come to thee and crave that boon which I feel assured you will not refuse me. My hand—my heart—my fortune will I lay before thee."

"And must you leave us soon?"

"Yes, before the sun reaches its meridian, the schooner and ship must part company, to sail in almost opposite directions. Believe me, Fanny, were it not my duty I would never leave thee."

"I do—I do believe thee, Edward," replied the lovely maiden, with energy.

"Go—my love shall not stand between thee and thy duty. Your purposes are truly noble, and I should feel guilty were I to endeavour to avert the course you have marked out."

"Generous creature, you give me happiness. Your last words will comfort me during my absence."

Their conversation was here interrupted by the approach of Captain Wingate, who desired to speak with Duvalle for a few moments on an urgent matter.

"Big Tom," said the captain, "who was arrested at your suggestion, desires to speak with you; he says that he is dying."

Edward went below where the burly sailor was confined, and the moment that he saw him he was convinced that he was not long for this world.

"Ah! I am glad you have come," said the dying sailor; "tell me, has the ' Spitfire ' been captured by the ship?"

"It is indeed so."

"I am happy to hear it. Oh, God! that I had lived any life but that of a pirate, I might now die in peace. What has become of Ringbold and the crew?"

"He is our prisoner—the crew are all dead."

"And why did you let him live?"

"To wring from him the secret he possesses in regard to myself."

"And has he divulged anything?"

"Yes—much. I have learned something of my own history."

"I could have told you of that, and intended to before I died, that it might have earned for me thy forgiveness."

"You can now narrate the story—the full corroboration of Ringbold's statement is what I most desire."

"Thank you—thank you," said the sailor; "I am glad that I can do the least good for you; for I have done you evil enough."

Big Tom gave Edward a detailed account of the galleon's capture, corroborating every particular of the statement as given by the pirate chief, but he could give him no knowledge respecting the long boat which was set adrift with the passengers. In continuation he said, "All I have told you is true, so help me Heaven!"

"Yes, I believe it, for it agrees with all I have heard from the villain Ringbold."

"And now," resumed the sailor, in a low and feeble voice, "remove the gold chain which encircles my neck."

Edward did as he was requested, and to his surprise he found attached to the chain a locket, set in diamonds, and containing a finely painted miniature of a lady of surpassing beauty and loveliness.

"That chain with my own hands I removed from your neck, before you were brought into the presence of the pirate chief. I was helmsman of the boat that picked up the box in which you were saved, and I bore you in my arms, while the men were rowing for the brigantine. I took it and concealed it about my person without the knowledge of my comrades, and have worn it constantly from that hour to this."

"Whose likeness do you suppose this to be?"

"It is your mother's! I had one look at her before she left the ship, and I know I cannot be mistaken ; besides I have often thought how much resemblance it bears to you."

"And can this, indeed, be the semblance of my dear mother?" ejaculated Edward, rapturously, as he gazed upon the picture and kissed it. "My mother— and yet so young and beautiful! Scarce seventeen summers could have passed over her head when she sat for this picture. There is a sweet smile resting upon her cherry-coloured lips ; and her large lustrous eyes beam lightly with hope and affection. Can it be true that so fair and pure a being could have been the mother of one like me? And yet I cannot doubt! Oh God!" continued he, clasping his hands and looking upward, "I trust that thou hast in thy divine wisdom, spared her life. Oh, lead me to her that I may love and bless her!"

"May Heaven grant your desires," exclaimed the dying man with a feeble utterance. "Forgive me—oh, forgive me ; and I die content."

The sailor reached out his hand, which Edward took kindly,—" I do forgive thee," he replied.

"God bless you !" were the last words of the dying mariner. His breathing grew short, and his pulse grew more feeble each moment—soon the death rattle sounded in his throat and he expired.

The captain was immediately summoned below, and he ordered, at Duvalle's request, that his body be prepared for burial in a like manner with those of the ship's company who had fallen in battle.

Silently our hero and Captain Wingate went upon deck. The sight of the corpse of one who had died a natural death, seemed to affect them more, than the sight of all the bodies of those who were slain in the heat of battle. They retired to the cabin, where Duvalle made known to the captain, his discoveries in regard to himself, as already known to our readers. But there is one matter, yet slightly enveloped in mystery, and which, perhaps, may be made clear through a portion of their conversation, which will be given in the course of another chapter.

——

CHAPTER VII.

INTERESTING CONVERSATION.—DEPARTURE OF THE PRIZE.—SHE IS CHASED BY AN ENGLISH FRIGATE.—ESCAPE, AND ARRIVAL AT HAVANA.—THE PRIZE IS BOARDED BY A REVENUE OFFICER.—QUERIES PROMPTLY ANSWERED.

"Your noble actions have convinced me," said Captain Wingate to Duvalle' in continuation of their interview, "that your plans were all matured before you registered your name as passenger on board of this ship."

"It is true," replied Duvalle ; "and this accounts for the muskets and ammunition which I sent on board with my luggage. I did not resolve to betray the pirates until after months of previous reflection. When I did resolve, I swore that it should be done the first opportunity ; and at the time Ringbold revealed to me his designs in regard to this ship, I eagerly accepted his proposition ; viz., that I should engage a passage in the "Sparta," and that Big Tom should ship as a foremast hand ; and, we were also instructed not only to contrive to render useless your ammunition but to spike your deck guns, that you might become an easy prey to the blood-thirsty and merciless hell-hounds, whom, with the aid of Heaven, we have exterminated."

"It was a perilous undertaking," remarked the captain.

"It seemed to me perfectly desperate ; but there was a silent monitor within me, which bade me go on. It was irresistible, and I obeyed, not dreaming that my plans could, by any means within my control, have proved so completely successful. I had two great objects in view ; one was to rid the sea of its greatest terror—the other was to penetrate the secret which the pirate chief had in his keeping concerning myself, and which I had often intreated in vain to gain from him."

"And you deserve honour and reward from the whole world for your great and glorious achievement ;" said Captain Wingate.

"Without your own personal aid," replied Duvalle, "I could do nothing."

"Pooh ! don't mention me again, only as one of the invincible thirty-five. But to return to business—how many men do you require to run the prize into Baltimore ?"

"Eight, if you can spare so many."

"You shall have them. Here are letters to my employers, together with the slight instructions necessary. I can trust everything to you. I shall hasten my voyage with all possible despatch, and I hope the return voyage will be completed, so that I may be with you at Baltimore in sixty or seventy days at the farthest."

"By this time all must be in readiness on board of the schooner, and I would not lose a minute unnecessarily. What shall be done with Ringbold?"

"Let him be removed to the ship; we can take care of him until we again reach home, when he shall be given up to the United States authorities."

A list of the men who were drafted to man the schooner was now handed to Edward, by the captain, when they both went upon deck and superintended the completion of the preparations for parting,

All was now in readiness, and Edward had taken leave of all on board, save one, a servant of whom now appeared on deck and gave him a slip of paper. It was a billet from Fanny Floyd, begging to see him one moment in the cabin with her father. He quickly obeyed the summons, but without breaking in upon their privacy, we shall merely say that their parting was an affectionate one, and whether the old gentleman really consented on this occasion to their union, shall be known hereafter.

The sails were hoisted—the helmsman stood at his post, and the order was given to cast off. As the two vessels separated, the crew cheered each other heartily, and so long as a signal could be discerned, they were made with white handkerchiefs from the quarter decks of the two vessels—we need not say by whom.

In three hours the "Sparta" and "Spitfire" were not within view of each other; every exertion being made on board of both vessels to make their respective ports of destination as speedily as possible.

It was ten o'clock, while the schooner was on her larboard tack, and going at the rate of eight knots (the wind having increased considerably) that she was hailed by a large frigate which suddenly hove in sight, and which was bearing down, with the wind on her quarter, towards the captured corsair. Duvalle, who was then below, suddenly appeared on deck, and espying a double-banked frigate, with an English ensign hoisted, within half a gunshot of him, hesitated for a few moments how to act. The pirate vessel had been so often described, he doubted not that she would be readily recognised by the frigate, and that, if he should allow her to be boarded by the British officers, all his assertions to the contrary might not convince them that she had within a few hours been captured by an American merchantman, and had been ordered home as a prize. Everything on board of the "Spitfire" was the same that was there before her capture, and no change was visible except in her crew. Our hero, although he knew that ultimately the truth could be ascertained, yet was satisfied that if once taken possession of by the Englishman, he and his crew would be subjected to much inconvenience, perhaps cruelty, and months in all probability would intervene, before the necessary evidence could be obtained to free them from a charge of piracy. With these views, he resolved to escape from her if possible, though her immediate proximity placed the schooner in a most hazardous position. One broadside, well-directed, from the frigate's double battery, would inevitably disable her.

A second time the schooner was hailed, and no answer was received. Duvalle, knowing that a shot would come next, ordered the long eighteens to be manned, that he might return the fire, and at the next moment to wear ship, in order to avoid the effects of a whole broadside which he reasonably anticipated, after setting the man-of-war at defiance. The sea around for a moment was illuminated, and the thirty-two pound shot whizzed over the deck of the "Spitfire," doing no injury in its flight. The fire was quickly returned, and the fore-top gallant-mast of the frigate fell by the board, and in another moment the "Spitfire" had borne away and now showed her heels to the enemy. But this manœuvre did not prevent John Bull from pouring from his double row of black teeth a full broadside upon the supposed corsair, and the shot flew over her deck like hail, doing some mischief to her upper spars and sails, which her young officer ordered immediately to be repaired as far as possible. The schooner gained fast upon the frigate, and an incessant fire was now kept up between them without doing much damage to either. Before midnight the "Spitfire" had managed to get beyond the reach of most of the frigate's guns; and as the chase had compelled him to run before the wind, and directly out of his course, Duvalle gave orders to brace up the yards and bring the schooner into the wind. This movement brought her again within range of the enemy's guns, but her intrepid officer trusted to the superior sailing qualities of his craft for escape, and at the same time to be nearing the port of destination. The frigate at first changed her course, only a point or two, but perceiving that her constant fire upon the schooner had not the desired effect, she, too hauled up into the wind and endeavoured to keep the weather gage. Her long thirty-two's were now put into requisition, and did considerable damage to the spars and sails of the schooner, and until repairs were made, they materially lessened her speed, yet, notwithstanding this she gained slowly upon the chase.

At sunrise the following morning, the "Spitfire" had gained sufficiently upon the pursuing vessel, so as to be entirely out of reach of her longest guns. The frigate, however, continued the pursuit, and as they were now near the West Indian islands, Duvalle resolved, that, under cover of the next night, he would run into one of the Spanish ports, where he hoped to find some American vessel of war, to which he might surrender the schooner, or ask for a convoy to the United States.

Accordingly as soon as as the shades of night entirely concealed the English frigate from view, he run into the port of Havana, and moored her among the thickest of the shipping in the harbor.

At daybreak, on the subsequent morning, the schooner "Vision" (the name of "Spitfire" having been removed during the night) was lying amid a fleet of vessels of almost every nation before the city of Havana. The Yankee flag was waving from her main truck, her sails were neatly furled, and everything about the craft presented a neat and trim appearance. About nine o'clock she was boarded by a revenue officer, as much from curiosity to examine the exterior of the beautiful vessel, as from a duty which he was bound to perform.

Duvalle was looking over the taffrail when the revenue boat came alongside, rowed by four men, the officer sitting in the stern acting as helmsman. As soon as he came upon the deck of the "Vision," (for by this name we shall henceforth call her), he approached our hero, and inquired, in the Spanish tongue, for permission to see her commander.

"I have that honor, sir," replied Duvalle.

"You, senor?" ejaculated the Spaniard, in surprise. "I took you rather for a cabin boy than the master."

"Notwithstanding, sir, I am for the present commander of this schooner."

"Whither bound?"

"To Baltimore."

"Where are your subordinate officers and crew?"

"They are all upon deck, sir, as you will perceive."

"What? an armed schooner and only eight men? Impossible!" said the officer, as he cast his eyes searchingly about the deck.

"I have spoken the truth, sir."

"How is it that your men wear not the uniform of the United States naval service?"

"The schoner belongs not to the United States Navy."

"Not to the United States Navy?" reiterated the officer, casting his eyes aloft and regarding our national ensign waving proudly from her masthead. "What means that flag?"

"Simply that she is an American vessel, sir!"

"Incredible! a private vessel, and carrying ten guns in time of peace;" exclaimed the revenue officer.

"It is, however strange it may appear, true."

"You will pardon me, senor, for being inquisitive; but being the revenue officer of this port, it is my imperative duty to ascertain more concerning this vessel. I would not be too officious, but it is so unusual to see an armed vessel of this class sailing under yonder flag on mercantile account, that I must make further inquiries. Is she a privateer?"

"No, sir."

"Is she a slaver?"

"No, sir."

"Then I must demand of you to produce your papers."

"I have none, sir, that I can produce with propriety. The only papers oard are hose of a pirate, formerly used by the desperado, Ringbold!"

The name of this renowned corsair chief struck the officer with awe. He looke upon the open and ingenuous countenance of the young commander with doubt and perplexity.

"Ringbold—the pirate? What mean you?"

"Simply, sir, that but a few days ago, that bold buccaneer and sixty of his desperadoes trod the deck of this vessel. She has since been captured, and is now the prize of the American merchant ship "Sparta!"

The officer was more and more astounded.

No. 5.

"What, a merchant ship capture this formidable craft and sixty men? What with, I pray?"

"With thirty-five seamen and passengers, armed with muskets, and two pieces of cannon!" replied our hero.

"It seems almost incredible! and yet from the appearance of your men and yourself, sir, I am bound to believe you. Can you show any proof other than the testimony of your men."

"I have letters, unsealed, from the first officer of the 'Sparta' to his employers at Baltimore, which, if you deem them necessary to peruse, I will place them immediately in your hands."

"This affair is so strange that I must ask you to go ashore with me and visit the governor of the Island, and let him judge of the matter himself."

"Thank you, sir, for your civility, and if you will allow yourself to be detained until I can prepare myself, I will accompany you with pleasure."

Our hero immediately repaired to his state-room, where he attired himself in a becoming suit for an audience with his excellency, and in the course of half an hour re-appeared on deck, and signified to the official dignitary that he was in readiness to accompany him.

"My duty compels me to leave one or more men on board of your vessel, until further orders from the governor."

"Your precaution, though unnecessary in this case, sir, I fully appreciate; the vessel may be considered under your surveillance until I have satisfied his excellency that I have represented correctly everything in regard to her."

The revenue officer having instructed one of his subordinates in the duty of ship-keeper until further orders, went on board his barge with Duvalle, and they were quickly rowed ashore, and proceeded directly to the palace of the governor.

Before entering, however, the booming of heavy cannon was heard, and on learning the cause, it was found that an English man-of-war had just arrived in port, and was firing a salute. Our young commander was apprehensive that this might be the frigate from which he had run away; but as he was in a Spanish port, he would seek protection from its authorities, if the Englishmen attempted to attack him.

CHAPTER VIII.

THE GOVERNOR AND HIS FAMILY.—DUVALLE VISITS THE PALACE, AND RELATES HIS RECENT ADVENTURES.—THE LETTERS.—GENEROSITY OF HIS EXCELLENCY.—FLORENCIA IS INTRODUCED TO DUVALLE.—ARRIVAL OF THE BRITISH NAVAL OFFICER.—HE DEMANDS THE "VISION" AS HIS PRIZE.—REFUSAL OF THE GOVERNOR.—HIS ANGER.—INTERFERENCE OF DUVALLE.—THE BRITISH OFFICER MAKES HIS EXIT WITH A FLEA IN HIS EAR.

THE governor of the Island of Cuba, at the time of which we write, was a noble gentleman of the old Castilian race, and, if he were considered somewhat despotic and arbitrary in the administration of the laws made for the island by old Spain, he certainly deserved much credit for his impartiality and magnanimity. He was a man of six feet in stature, finely proportioned, and possessed a noble and dignified bearing, especially in the presence of his subjects. He was about forty-five years of age, though he appeared somewhat younger—his hair being of a glossy black, and his eye retaining all the fire and expression of youth.

The wife of his excellency was some five years younger, of remarkably light complexion, and large lustrous eyes, and although forty years had passed over her head, she yet retained much of the beauty which she could boast of in her more youthful days. She was a native of Louisiana, and was married in New Orleans, where her husband made her acquaintance. They afterwards moved to the land of his nativity, and some years afterwards, being noble by birth, and possessing every qualification for any responsible station, he was appointed by his king, governor of the Island of Cuba, whither he removed soon after his appointment. They were blessed with one child, a daughter, about seventeen years of age, of great beauty and sweetness. Florencia, for this was her Christian name, resembled her beautiful mother, in a great degree. She was at once the joy and pride of her noble parents, and commanded the love and admiration of all who enjoyed her acquaintance.

Florencia, on the morning of which we write, was standing with her mother in the balcony of the palace which overlooked the picturesque and animated harbour of Havana. The sun was shining brightly, but the cool and invigorating breezes from the sea rendered the atmosphere less oppressive than usual. Hundreds of flags and streamers of various nations, were waving from the mast-head of the shipping, and the " yo, heave ho !" of the sailors broke merrily upon the ears of the two females, who regarded the scene with sensations of delight. Florencia and her mother had been remarking upon the more beautiful vessels of the great fleet which spread out before them, and the symmetrical proportions of the schooner with the star-spangled banner flying at her mast-head had not escaped their attention, when the governor joined them upon the balcony. His eye immediately caught sight of the American, when he exclaimed,—

"By San Iago ! yon clipper-built craft looks like a Baltimorean ! It is a rare sight to see one of that class of vessels in our harbour. She must have been sent here for an especial purpose. Hand me my glass, daughter, I must have a nearer view of her."

Florencia with a fawn-like step ran to obey her father's wishes. In a moment she returned bearing the telescope which the Governor placed to his eye, and for a long time scrutinised the vessel.

"She carries ten guns, and yet I can perceive but eight men upon her decks, besides a youth who is looking over her side. The men are dressed like common American sailors, and she therefore cannot belong to the navy."

" A boat is approaching her," said Florencia.

" It is the revenue boat," replied his excellency ; "and if I mistake not, Senor Garcia, himself, our first revenue officer, has charge of her. Yes, he has boarded the American, and is now talking with the young man aft. I never saw a more perfect model of a sailing craft in my life," continued he, laying aside his glass. " I cannot imagine what she is, or for what purpose she is here."

" Perhaps she bears despatches for the United States consul," replied the governor's wife. "Surely she comes on no hostile errand with a handful of men."

" It is very probable," replied his excellency. " Our indefatigable officer will soon inform me."

While the governor and his wife were conversing upon the loveliness of the morning and the gay and animated appearance of the harbour, Dona Florencia was looking through the telescope, watching every movement on board of the schooner. She had observed the young man go below, and as the revenue officer still tarried on deck, she thought he had gone to call the commander of the schooner. When the young officer again appeared on deck, genteelly attired, he became an object of interest to her, inasmuch as she thought that he must be the captain of the craft, for he seemed to be giving orders to his men, and had evidently prepared himself for accompanying his official visitor to the shore.

" Father," said she, in sweet and gentle tones, " the young man whom you saw, is the first officer of the handsome vessel."

" How know you that, my daughter ?" interrogated the governor.

" He has been giving orders to his men ; and is now coming ashore in company with Senor Garcia."

" Ah ! then they will be here shortly. My word for it, daughter, he is not the commander ; most likely the owner's son."

"Then why did he give orders?"

"How is it possible that you should know that he did? Your sense of hearing certainly cannot be sufficiently acute to enable you to hear at a distance of at least two hundred rods."

"Oh! but then you know I could tell by his gestures. I saw him making motions to his men, and could almost see his lips move."

"Then I dare say, daughter, you have already discovered whether he is good or ill looking?"

"Yes, father, he is decidedly handsome," said Florencia, frankly, and with a smiling countenance. "I never saw a more graceful figure, unless it be you excellency's!"

"Tut, tut, Flora," said her mother archly, "you will make your father vain in his years of manhood, if you pay him such compliments."

"There is little danger, madam," said his excellency; "but if you had complimented my person so highly twenty years ago, it would undoubtedly have added considerably to my pride. We must keep an eye on our daughter," continued he, facetiously; "she is fast losing her heart through a telescope."

"No fear, father," answered the senorita; "I have only magnified the young man's perfections."

Meanwhile the boat was fast approaching the shore, and shortly after Senor Garcia and Duvalle had landed, they were announced to his excellency the governor.

"Shall we not be present at the interview, father?" inquired Donna Florencia.

"No, daughter, should I require your services, I will send for you," replied his excellency, as he left his wife and daughter, and repaired to the audience chamber of the palace.

"*Buen venido*, Senor Garcia!" exclaimed the governor, as the revenue officer entered the room, followed by Duvalle.

"*Muchas gracias!*" replied Senor Garcia "Senor Duvalle, commander of the American schooner 'Vision,'" continued he, introducing our hero.

"Welcome, stranger!" said the governor, approaching him, and taking the youth by the hand. "You are young to have the command of an armed vessel."

"The command is but a temporary one," replied Duvalle. "I am merely commissioned to carry the schooner safely into the port of Baltimore."

"Yes, your excellency," added Senor Garcia, "the schooner which he has the honour of commanding, is a prize to an American merchantman."

"A prize?" interrupted the governor; "what mean you?"

"You will perceive by these letters, which I have deemed prudent to place in your hands for perusal, that this vessel is none other than the one formerly commanded by the terror of the ocean,—the pirate Ringbold!

"Santa Maria! and has the bloody monster met with his just deserts?" ejaculated the governor, looking with intensity upon the noble countenance of the youth.

"His crew have to a man been destroyed!" answered Duvalle; "and he himself is a prisoner on board of the merchant ship "Sparta." He will be taken to the United States, where he will most undoubtedly meet with his just reward."

"No, by San Iago, such a devil cannot be punished this side of the infernal regions!" said the governor in an agitated manner. "None have better reasons than myself for wishing the bloody hell-hound the worst of punishments! Would to God that it was left to me to inflict the pains he deserves on earth! There could be no torture invented too keen for the monster's body; and though I never beheld a punishment in my life, when I did not feel a pity for the person on whom it was inflicted, yet, I could rejoice heartily to witness this horrible and merciless villain writhing in all the agonies of the most extreme torture!"

While the governor was speaking, big drops of sweat stood on his noble brow, and his whole frame quivered with the violence of his feelings. At length, partially composing himself, he said,—

"Excuse me, gentlemen, for allowing my indignant feelings to gain a momentary ascendancy over me."

Saying which, he bade his visitors to be seated, and commenced perusing the letters and other documents which had been brought from the schooner.

"The account of this capture is truly as astounding as the conflict was bloody," at length said the governor, rising and addressing Duvalle, "and I perceive that to you belongs the honour of this almost incredible capture! I feel proud of your acquaintance, sir," continued he, taking the hand of our hero. "None have greater reasons for gratitude to you than myself, and how shall I show the sincerity of my feelings?"

"Your excellency is kind," answered Duvalle; "but none have gained so much by this victory as myself, and therefore your approval of my conduct, as well as that of the world at large, will more than repay me.

"By *San Diego*," exclaimed his excellency; "I cannot let you depart without bestowing upon you a slight token of my gratitude and esteem."

"You have already done me greater honour than my merits deserve," replied our hero, as the governor left the apartment.

After an absence of a few moments he returned, bearing in his hand a magnificent Damascus sword, the hilt enriched by gold and precious stones. His daughter followed him, who was immediately introduced to the handsome young stranger. There was something in the countenance of the graceful Florencia, which sank deeper into the heart of Edward Duvalle, than its surpassing loveliness. Was it love? Had she, too, as well as the beautiful Fanny Floyd struck the chords of affection? or were the sensations which the sight of the Spanish maiden produced in his bosom, of a different, of a loftier, of a holier nature? There was a powerful feeling pervading his whole soul, of which he was conscious, but for which he could not account. His eyes were riveted upon the maiden with glowing intensity, nor did he remove them until the governor again approached him, and broke the spell by which he seemed bound for many moments. Said his excellency,—

"Allow me, my brave youth, to present you with this sword, in token of the great service you have rendered, not only the Spanish nation, but all the civilised commercial nations of the earth!"

Our hero was so embarrassed by the presence of Donna Florencia, that he almost disregarded the words of the governor. He received the magnificent present in silence; when she came forward, and taking from her neck a massive gold chain, to which was appended a small gold cross, studded with diamonds, she wound it around his neck, and bade him wear it as a testimonial of her esteem for the great service he had done her father.

With a modest grace he bowed his head, while she bestowed the gift upon him, and placed his hand upon his heart, in token of his gratitude, for he was too much overcome to utter a single sentence.

Had custom permitted, he would have folded his arms about the beautiful creature, and pressed her to his bosom. Strange as it may appear, it was a pure and holy impulse that prompted the desire! What was it? We shall see anon.

The audience now being at an end, Duvalle prepared to take his departure, not, however, before extending an invitation to the governor, and to his family, if they desired it, to visit and examine the piratical craft. Just as Duvalle and the revenue officer were exchaning a parting salute, the door opened, and an English naval officer was announced, who entered the room abruptly, and in great excitement. As Duvalle mistrusted that it was the commander of the frigate who had chased him, he tarried to make explanation if necessary.

"Your excellency will pardon me," said he, "for my business is of an urgent nature. I am commander of his Britannic majesty's frigate 'Thunderer,' and have been for several days in chase of a piratical schooner, which is now moored within sight of your palace! I ask permission to take possession of her as lawful prize, in the name of his majesty, George the Fourth!"

"You forget, Sir Stranger, that this is a Spanish port," replied the governor, calmly.

"Nevertheless, and with all due respect to your excellency, I claim her as the prize of the frigate 'Thunderer.' She but last night escaped us, and took refuge immediately under the guns of your castle!"

"I cannot grant your request," said the governor, with the utmost coolness, not liking the blustering airs of the Englishman.

"What, sir, do you positively deny my request?" said the British captain, in menacing tones.

"Most positively!"

"And allow your port to become a place of refuge for every bloody corsair who desires to enter it?"

"I know my duty, and shall follow it."

"And I know mine," added the Englishman, "and shall immediately forward despatches to my government, giving information of this monstrous violation of the laws of nations."

"You have my permission to do that, and also permission to leave my palace!" said the governor, unable longer to restrain his indignation at the officer's blustering manner. "If you have any other business with me, let it be done through a substitute, who can demean himself with becoming propriety."

"Your insolence is insufferable!" replied the Englishman, his face livid with rage.

"A more polite language would better become you," said the governor, with the most imperturbable coolness; "or if you cannot keep a little more civil by persuasion, other measures must be resorted to."

When the governor had thus spoken, the face of the Englishman assumed a livid hue; his eyes were bloodshot, his brow lowered, his muscles writhed, and in a voice almost inarticulate with passion, he ejaculated,—

"Do you dare, sir, to speak to me, an officer in his majesty's service, in this manner? Do you dare to menace me with your threats? If that be the case," said he, with increased ire, "draw and defend yourself."

It was fortunate that the governor was not so irascible as the English officer, or bloodshed might have, and most probably would have ensued from the language used; but as it was the governor in the same undisturbed, almost a pathetic manner which he evinced in everything, answered,—

"Your rank as an officer and a gentleman prevents me forming the conclusion from your words that I should otherwise be inclined to construe them into. Sheath your sword, sir, again, and draw it in future in a better cause."

During the short time that it took the governor to speak these few words, the choller of the English officer seemed to increase, rather than diminish. He first looked at the governor, and then at Duvalle, but observing the calm demeanour of them both, he seemed to be censuring himself in his own mind for his hastiness, and therefore said,—

"I must apologise for my conduct to you, sir, which has been rather unwarrantable."

Having made this concession, the governor likewise offered an apology to the Englishman; and thus the altercation appeared to end.

During all this time Duvalle had remained perfectly neutral, not taking the slightest notice of either party, acting on the principle that the interference of a third party always makes matters worse than they otherwise would have been. He now stepped forward, and said to the English officer,—

"There appears to be some mistake here."

"There does, indeed," said the officer.

"I dare say it can soon be explained, and that in the most amicable manner," he added, glancing first at the officer, who wondered what he was about to say, and then at the governor. "If it can be that is all that can possibly be desired," he said addressing Duvalle.

There was then a short pause, during which neither seemed inclined to give the required explanation.

"Will you allow me to explain this matter?" asked Duvalle of the governor, in a courteous and persuasive manner.

"Certainly! I cannot refuse, as you are probably somewhat interested in this matter."

"Do I address," said Duvalle, approaching the angry Englishman, "the first officer of a double banked English frigate, which, for the few past days has been in pursuit of a small schooner, carrying ten guns and only eight men?"

The officer looked upon the interrogator with surprise.

"I have been in chase of a formidable pirate vessel," said he, under the command of the noted Ringbold, and it is said that he has under him sixty men!"

"And did your ship sustain the loss of a fore-top gallant-mast by a shot from the pirate?" again questioned Duvalle.

"Yes, besides the frigate sustained considerable injury in the hull from the incessant and well directed fire of the schooner."

"Indeed! I trust you lost no lives?"

"Not a man," answered the Englishman, wondering at the inquisitiveness and knowledge of the handsome young stranger.

"It is well," answered Duvalle; "and now to prevent any difficulty between his excellency the governor, and yourself, I will confess that the schooner you speak of, I have the honour to command."

"You?" ejaculated the frigate's first officer.

"Yes, you have deceived yourself in regard to the present character of the schooner. That she was once the vessel you believe, is very true, but, sir, owing to the good fortune and bravery of the crew and passengers of an American merchantman, mounting but two guns, the formidable pirate has been captured, and I have been commissioned to carry her into port."

"Incredible!" exclaimed the Englishman.

"Wonderful!" added the governor, ironically, "that the schooner with only eight men, should have made a successful resistance, and afterwards succeed in making her escape from His Britannic Majesty's frigate 'Thunderer,' under the command of such a valorous officer."

The Englishman felt the keenness of the governor's remark, and without making a reply, he bit his lip, turned upon his heel and left the palace.

"Stay one moment," said the governor to our hero; "what, did you really engage with this chop-fallen braggadocia Englishman, and shoot away the frigate's fore-top gallant-mast?"

"We did, your excellency."

"By San Iago! I like you all the better for that deed. Then the saucy fellow tried to capture a prize instead of a pirate?"

"He did, your Excellency; but the fellow thought he was doing his king service."

"Why did you wish to escape him?"

"I feared that he might doubt me, and carry me into port," answered Duvalle. "At all events, I preferred rather to trust to the superior sailing qualities of the 'Vision,' than to the doubtful clemency of one of these British ocean monarchs."

"And you did well, my brave youth!" exclaimed the governor. "I shall do myself the honour to visit your vessel this afternoon."

"The honour will give me great pleasure," replied our hero. "I shall not fail to get the ship in a fit condition for your reception, and if you choose to bring any friends with you, I can only say that I shall be equally pleased with their company."

"I am truly obliged to you," replied the governor, shaking him heartily by the hand, "and shall not fail to avail myself of your offer."

"Do so."

"I will, you may depend."

"Perhaps, among those whom I am to be honoured with, you will bring your pretty daughter here with you."

Duvalle then smiled affectionately upon Donna Florencia, who blushed deeply under his scrutinising glance.

"Shall I not accompany you, father?" asked Donna Florencia, who began to feel a greater interest in the stranger than could have been supposed at first sight.

"Yes, my daughter."

"And mother, too?"

"If it be her pleasure."

Duvalle again bidding them good morning, took his departure, and repaired immediately on board of the "Vision;" and in anticipation of the governor's visit, gave orders to have the beautiful craft put in the best possible trim, and to make preparation for the proper reception of their illustrious visitors.

No sooner had Duvalle departed, and the governor was alone with his daughter, than he said to her,—

"And so you seem to have awakened as much interest in Duvalle, now that he has seen you, as he did in you before you had seen him."

Florencia smiled, but returned no answer to her father's remark. Then he continued,—

"Now don't blush, child, there's nothing to be ashamed of; but it's very singular that you should have spied him out at such a distance, and then to be brought together in this manner. Florencia," he continued, "it strikes me that I have seen Duvalle before, but where I am sure I cannot tell."

"Indeed, father," said his daughter, her eyes brightening at the pleasing thought of her father, perhaps, being able to recollect where.

"Yes, I am almost certain of that—I seem to know his voice. Let me consider. "No," he continued, in an abstracted manner, and pressing his hand to his temples, as if to assist his memory, "I can't remember where; but when we visit the ship this afternoon I'll question him."

"Do so, father," said Florencia.

The governor then quitted the room to attend to some business which was urgent, leaving his daughter absorbed in her own contemplations.

CHAPTER IX.

CONCLUSION.

It was a lovely afternoon in the month of September, the sun was yet about two hours above the horizon, when the signal was given for the departure of the governor from the quay. As if by magic, the beautiful clipper "Vision" was dressed in the flags of every commercial nation; and from her guns a salute was fired which made the welkin ring with their roar. The beautiful silken canopied barge of the governor, propelled by twelve oarsmen, soon came alongside; and his excellency, with his wife and daughter, was received with due courtesy by the young and gallant officer of the "Vision," and escorted to the magnificently furnished cabin of the schooner, when the governor introduced to him his wife, and the lovely senorita, whom he had seen at the palace, gracefully saluted him.

The same impulses which had agitated our hero on first seeing Donna Florencia, now moved him as before, and on beholding the face of her mother, it was increased. He seemed confused beyond measure, and was at a loss how to act.

Attributing the young officer's apparent bashfulness and confused manner to the presence of ladies, the governor talked rapidly concerning the beauties of the vessel, of her remarkable capture, the richness of her cabin, and other matters for the purpose of dispelling the embarrassment which so suddenly overcame him.

Duvalle was not the only one who was moved by impulses, the cause of which they could not divine. The wife of his Excellency, on first beholding the form

and features of our hero, gazed abstractedly upon him; her daughter, too, Donna Florencia, with an interest, amounting to admiration, watched his every movement. The governor's affability and openness of manner, soon partially dispelled this unknown influence, and each, recovering in a degree their wonted confidence, entered into conversation with increased animation.

No. 6.

Duvalle gave a whole history of the capture of the pirate, and of the chase of the frigate, keeping himself, however, as the chief actor, far in the back ground. He then commenced showing them many valuable articles, which formerly belonged to the pirates; and among other things he took from the iron chest the casket of jewels, of which we have before spoken, and opening it before them displayed its riches.

"*Santa madre Deios!*" exclaimed the senora, extremely agitated; "what do I behold! Look! Do you not recognise these, your excellency," said she, directing his attention to the jewels.

"*San Diego!*" exclaimed he; "they look like the jewels that were——"

"They are the same!" interrupted the Senora. "I pray you, Senor Duvalle, tell me; know you more of these jewels than the mere fact of their being taken from the pirate?"

"Yes, madam, I know much; they nearly concern me."

"Concern thee!" reiterated the senora, "your name is——"

"I am at present known by the name of Edward Duvalle," he interrupted. "Of my true name I am not positive, but I believe it to be San Malo."

"And these jewels?" ejaculated the governor, regarding him with wonder.

"Are mine! They were taken from me when a child; together with this chain and miniature," replied Duvalle, taking them from his neck, and handing them to the senora.

"He is!—he is my son! my long lost, darling boy!" screamed the senora, and fell overcome with joy into the arms of Duvalle.

"My mother! my dear mother! I thank God that I have found thee at last!" exclaimed Edward. "And thee, too, my father! Oh, my God! can this be true? or am I dreaming?"

"My son! my son!" added the governor, "my brave—my noble boy! By what miracle have we found thee at last?"

Donna Florencia stood regarding this scene, amazed in perplexity and doubt. She had been told when a child that she would have had a little brother had he lived, and a faint reminiscence of that knowledge still lingered like a long remembered dream in her mind. That he should be still among the living was a miracle too wonderful for her comprehension; yet she had heard her parents, wild exclamations, had seen all that had passed, and she stood trembling like a leaf, uncertain how to act.

The first ebullition of joy having subsided, the elated youth encountered the beautiful senorita, who stood before him, when his excellency with joy exclaimed,—

"Florencia, your brother! Eustaquio, your sister!"

"My dear sister!"

"My dear brother!" were the only exclamations of the son and daughter, as they embraced and kissed each other with all the fervency of a holy passion.

Mutual explanations were now entered into, and before the whole party had left the schooner for the palace, each was acquainted with the history of the other.

Our hero accompanied his father and mother to the palace, and after remaining two or three weeks, enjoying more happiness each hour than he had experienced during his whole life, he told the governor that he had made a promise to take the prize into Baltimore; and until he should fulfil it, there still remained something unaccomplished to complete his happiness.

His excellency reluctantly permitted him to depart; but out of regard to his safety, he despatched an armed brig after him with instructions to act as a convoy to the prize, without allowing his son to know of it, and to remain in the port of Baltimore, until it was his pleasure to return, and then to solicit him to take passage in the brig.

In eleven days after the "Vision" sailed, she had arrived in the harbour of Baltimore. Her commander immediately afterward reported himself to the owners of the Sparta, who were amazed at the contents of the despatches; nor could they realise the truth of them until they visited the prize in person. For several days our hero was toasted and lionised by those interested, and by the few to. whom the whole affair had been made known.

The brig, which had been sent as a convoy to the prize, or rather, to her young commander, although a tolerably fast sailor, was far outstripped by the schooner in their passage from Havana, and she was not reported in the harbour of Baltimore, until eight days after the " Vision" had been moored before the city. The captain of the brig immediately reported himself to San Malo, and informed him that the brig was subject to his orders.

On the fifth day after the arrival of the convoy, our hero was rejoiced to see the " Sparta" moving majestically up the Chesapeake Bay. His impatience would not permit him to await her arrival at the anchorage ground, he therefore procured a boat, and was soon alongside the noble old ship, for which he had quite an affection. He was joyfully greeted by Captain Wingate, and by those were on board at the time of the victory over the corsair. They narrated to each other a history of the incidents that had transpired since their parting—that of young San Malo is already in the possession of our readers; that of Captain Wingate's was marked by nothing particularly interesting except that Mr. Floyd and the beautiful Fanny had both unexpectedly returned, the former having partially recovered his health.

It having reached the ears of Fanny Floyd that our young hero was actually on board of the ship, she adjusted the curls of her beautiful hair, and other trifling matters of the toilet, and made her appearance in the main cabin, from her state room, just as he entered from the deck. If possible she looked more blooming and beautiful than ever. They being together for a moment or two alone, it is not to be marvelled at, nor is it a matter at all reprehensible, that they rushed into each other's arms, and snatched from each other's lips the first kiss of love. There must, of course, in all these matters be a first time, and why not, very properly, on this occasion. It would have all done very well had they been satisfied with one embrace, or one kiss, but they, like all indiscreet lovers, repeated it, I know not how many times, until they were surprised, in the very act of kissing each other, by Mr. Floyd himself, who suddenly appeared in the cabin to the utter confusion of both.

Mr. Floyd approached the young man, gave him his hand and evinced great pleasure in seeing him again.

"Come here, you little minx," said he to his daughter, playfully. " I have observed enough to satisfy me ; you love this noble youth, do you not? Now, you might as well confess it, and not blush so."

" Why, papa, I——"

" Come, come, no mincing the matter, you might as well out with it, frankly and boldly at once."

" Well, papa, I suppose I must say—say—yes !"

" Yes, you jade, you couldn't have said anything else, if you had tried—no, would have choked you. And you love my daughter?" continued he, addressing the young man.

" With all my heart !" he replied.

"Spoken like a man !" said Mr. Floyd, as he took Fanny's hand and placed it in that of her lover's. There, take her. She is a good girl, and I have got a fortune in reserve for her. God bless you ! May you ever be happy !"

In two weeks after this scene on board of the " Sparta," we noticed the following marriage in one of the papers :—

" Married at St. Inigoes, on the 24th inst., by the Rev. Thomas'———, CARLOS EUSTAQUIO SAN MALO, only son of the Governor of the Island of Cuba, to MISS FANNY MARIA, only daughter of Hon. Francis Floyd, of St. I."

* * * * * * *

Captain Wingate and the commander of the Spanish armed brig were the only guests present at the solemn ceremony of the marriage of his young friend, other than the near relatives of Mr. Floyd. In the course of a week after their marriage, the young bride and bridegroom embarked on board the Spanish vessel which his excellency had sent out as a convoy.

There was great rejoicing on their arrival at Havanah. The governor gave a magnificent levee in honour of the occasion, which was attended by many hundreds of the noble and aristrocratic of the Island.

The bloody pirate, Ringbold, was tried, condemned and executed in the city of Baltimore, and his body was afterwar s given up to the surgeons for dissection. We understand that his skull can be seen at the Museum of that city, among the other "thousand and one' curiosities which are there on exhibition.

Thus ends the romance of "The Corsair, or the Foundling of the Sea;" and should any of our readers affect to disbelieve its main incidents, the author stands ready to substantiate them.

THE END.